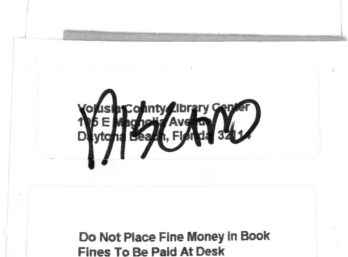

A KILLING IN KIOWA

G·K
Hall
&Cº

Also by Lewis B. Patten
in Large Print:

Death Stalks Yellowhorse
Gun Proud
Guns at Gray Butte
Home is the Outlaw
The Orphans of Coyote Creek
Prodigal Gunfighter
Pursuit
Ride a Crooked Trail
The Ruthless Range
The Scaffold at Hangman's Creek
Tincup in the Storm Country
Track of the Hunter
The Trail of the Apache Kid
Trail to Vicksburg
Villa's Rifles

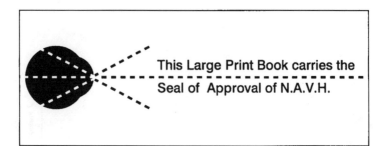

This Large Print Book carries the
Seal of Approval of N.A.V.H.

A KILLING IN KIOWA

Lewis B. Patten

G.K. Hall & Co. • **Thorndike, Maine**

Copyright © 1972 by Lewis B. Patten

Published in 2001 by arrangement with Golden West Literary Agency.

G.K. Hall Large Print Western Series.

The text of this Large Print edition is unabridged.
Other aspects of the book may vary from the original edition.

Set in 16 pt. Plantin.

Printed in the United States on permanent paper.

Library of Congress Cataloging-in-Publication Data

Patten, Lewis B.
    A killing in Kiowa / by Lewis B. Patten.
      p. cm.
    ISBN 0-7838-9352-3 (lg. print : hc : alk. paper)
    1. Sheriffs — Fiction. 2. Large type books. I. Title.
PS3566.A79 K45 2001
  813′.54—dc21   00-053848

A KILLING IN KIOWA

CHAPTER

1

Daisy Middleton left the saloon at one, a little early, before the last customer had gone. She stood motionless in the cool night air for a moment, before turning toward the two-room house, a block down and a block over, that she rented from the owner of the saloon, Brock Davidson, for fifteen dollars a month.

She had a headache and she was tired. It was a hell of a way to make a living, she thought, for a moment envying the town's respectable women at home in their beds with their husbands beside them, and their children asleep in their upstairs rooms. Impatiently, she turned toward home. This was the only thing she knew, the only thing she had known since she turned fifteen. She was twenty-five now, but in the glaring, harsh light of day, she looked ten years older than that. Night was kinder to her because it hid the disillusionment in her eyes, hid the wrinkles that were beginning to show themselves on her forehead and at her throat, hid the occasional traces of bitterness that showed themselves at the corners of her mouth.

She hustled drinks in the saloon, but if a man had a dollar and wanted her, she would climb the stairs with him at any hour of the day or night to the room Brock Davidson provided for that purpose at the head of the stairs. There used to be three girls in the Ace High Saloon, but that had been when the trail herds were hitting Kiowa, when there had been more single men drifting through. Now she was the only one. She got all the business. Trouble was, she had to give fifty cents out of every dollar to Brock. And what with the hard times, she lived and that was all.

Wearily, she walked toward home and, passing the alley, heard their footsteps coming before she saw them, before she even heard them speak. Men were her business, and she was not afraid. Not even when she saw that there were four of them. Not even when she saw how young they were, how clumsy and how drunk, and knew what they meant to do.

The four were too young to buy drinks in the saloon. Carl Eggers was sixteen, Frank Avila, seventeen. Orvie Gunderson and Marv Shapiro were only fifteen, but both would be sixteen in the fall. Marv Shapiro was the banker's son, and it had been he who slipped into the unlocked alley door of the saloon and stole the quart bottle of whiskey they had finished earlier.

None of the four was really drunk, but all were feeling reckless and wild, each itching to show off before the other three, each feeling a heady something that was new and that, for tonight, passed for the manhood none of the four would achieve for several years. They had been talking about women, and all four wanted one. They had heard Daisy coming along the silent and deserted street several moments before she actually reached the mouth of the alleyway.

Not a one of them would have dared accost Daisy had he been alone. The presence of the other three gave each a courage he would not otherwise have possessed. Tonight they were a miniature mob. They did not think of Daisy as an individual like themselves, with feelings and fears and weaknesses and strengths. She was only the whore from the saloon. For a dollar she'd take on anyone. Well, tonight she was going to take on all four of them. And she wasn't going to get a dime for it.

Orvie Gunderson was the biggest of the four. He reached her first and grabbed her by the arm. Frank Avila reached her next, put an arm around her waist and slid his other hand into the neckline of her dress. Marv whispered urgently, "For God's sake, Orvie, drag her back in here! Do you want the whole damn town to see?"

Avila began to drag her back into the dark alley, and when she struggled, Marv picked up her feet. He was trembling all over now with a kind of excitement he had never experienced before. His breath came in ragged gasps, as if he had been running hard.

9

At first, Daisy struggled only halfheartedly. Now, as she felt herself lifted, as she felt her blouse torn by a trembling, eager hand, anger made her scream.

A dirty hand instantly clamped itself over her mouth. Other hands ripped at her clothes, brutal in their clumsy eagerness. She bit the hand over her mouth savagely, and when it was jerked away, screamed furiously again.

A fist struck her in the mouth and she tasted blood. She knew she ought to stop struggling, knew now that she might be badly beaten if she did not.

But she had a headache and she was tired. And she was angry at their callous disregard, both for her personally, and for her clothes. She continued to struggle, but she was no match for them. They threw her down into the alley dirt and were on her like a pack of wolves.

Arnold Means finished his beer a moment after Daisy left. He said good-night to Brock Davidson and stepped out into the cool June night. Turning his head, he saw Daisy walking wearily down the street. She turned the corner and disappeared.

Arnold hated going home. His wife had died six months before, but even six months had not dulled the ache of sleeping alone in the bed they once had shared, of waking to an empty house, of being so terribly lonely every minute he spent at home.

Arnold Means owned the hardware store. His days were occupied, and there was a fairly constant stream of people going in and out of his store. But when quitting time came, when it was time to go home once more to that empty house, a depression he had never experienced while Sally was alive would come over him. Some nights he simply could not force himself to go home after work. He would take supper at the hotel or in the restaurant. Afterward he would go to the saloon, where he would spend the evening, drinking enough beer to make him sleep when he did go home, but not enough to make him drunk.

Sometimes he would watch Daisy Middleton out of the corner of an eye, wanting her, needing her, knowing that for a dollar he could go upstairs with her. And all the time he watched and wanted her, he hated himself for his dis- loyalty to Sally. She hadn't been in the ground six months, and here he was wanting to replace her with a whore that for a dollar anyone could have.

He turned toward home reluctantly, stopping when he heard what sounded like a scream from the direction in which Daisy Middleton had gone. He listened a moment, then with a faint shrug continued on toward home.

The second scream stopped him in his tracks, telling him the first had not been his imagination after all. He glanced briefly at the saloon, thinking maybe he ought to get Brock Davidson's help, then ran down the street without asking for it.

When he rounded the corner, the street lay empty in front of him. Daisy had disappeared. He stopped, thinking again that he had imagined it, that she was already safely in her house.

But the house, which he could see from here, stayed dark. No light flickered in its windows, and he knew she would surely have lighted a lamp immediately after going in the door.

The alley, he thought. He glanced back toward the saloon, knowing he ought to get Brock Davidson's help in this. Then he heard a muffled cry and knew there wasn't time. He ran toward the alley mouth alone.

Arnold Means had not been in a fight since grade school. He'd only been in one fight then, and he'd lost it when he was knocked down with blood streaming from his nose. He didn't know now what he was getting into, but he didn't hesitate. Daisy had screamed. She was a woman and she needed help. He was the only man who had heard her scream, and it was up to him to provide that help. It was that simple. He was scared, as scared as he had time to be, but he went on anyway.

He reached the alley mouth. It was darker in there, but the stars provided a little light. He could see movement, that of several people, and he could hear the grunting, scuffing sounds of struggle. He yelled, "Hey! What the hell's going on?"

He was not answered, except for a helpless, pain-filled outcry, obviously a woman's voice. He hesitated only an instant, now deeply afraid, then plunged into the alley yelling, "Get the hell away from her! Leave her alone!"

They were only fifty feet or so back from the alley mouth, and he reached them almost immediately. He heard a harsh, youthful voice say, "Get the son-of-a-bitch out of here."

The voice sounded like that of Marv Shapiro and Arnold asked, "Marv? Is that you?" Then someone collided with him and knocked him off his feet. It was a shoulder that had struck him, squarely in the belly, and it knocked the wind out of him. Gasping, trying to regain his breath, he lay there helplessly. He felt kicks landing in his ribs and against his rump and thighs and back. A boot slammed against his ear and made his head ring.

Another voice, unmistakable because of its Spanish accent, said thickly, "Hurry up, Marv. It's my turn next." Another kick struck his head and he felt consciousness slipping away from him. He managed to croak, "Frank! Help me, Frank!" Avila occasionally worked for him in the hardware store, and he knew the boy's voice as well as he knew his own.

But there was something frenzied now about their kicks. Two of them had been recognized, and they knew that tomorrow they would have to pay for what they had done tonight. A kick landed squarely in Arnold's mouth, breaking teeth, bringing the salty taste of blood. Another struck him viciously above the ear, and this was the last one he felt. Consciousness slipped away, and although he tried to hang onto it, he failed.

They kept on kicking him for several moments, until they realized that he hadn't moved for quite a while. They stopped, then, and stood over him, breathing hard. Marv Shapiro, who had not participated, pushed himself away from Daisy and struggled to his feet. He saw Arnold's motionless body on the ground and said, "What the hell did you do to him?"

Daisy crawled toward the concealment of a sagging fence, clutching the tattered rags of her clothes. She wasn't badly hurt, but now for the first time she was scared. One of the boys said, "Jesus, we better get out of here!"

The passion that had driven them to what they had done was gone. Now, suddenly, they were only boys again, scared boys who had done something even they did not fully understand.

Leaving their victims, they ran down the alley, turned the corner into the street, and disappeared.

For a time Daisy crouched against the fence, trying without success to arrange her clothes so that they covered her. The man lying in the alley hadn't moved. She struggled to her feet and went to him. She knelt and shook him, but his body stayed limp.

She knew, instinctively, that he was badly hurt. She ran down the alley to the street. She stumbled to the corner.

She saw Brock Davidson in front of the saloon, locking up. She screamed, and in her scream was all the terror she felt for the man who had come to her aid and who was hurt because of it.

Brock turned, saw her, and immediately came running toward her. He saw her condition and said, "Holy God! Who. . . . ?"

She realized that she was screaming incoherently at him, and she didn't care. "Never mind me! Someone tried to help me, and he's in that alley, maybe dead!"

He headed for the alley with Daisy following. Blindly, he ran up the alley and knelt beside Arnold Means. He put his hand lightly on Arnold's chest, felt its faint rise and fall. Rising, he turned, "Go home and get something on. Then get the sheriff. I'll get Doc McNab."

He ran from the alley and up the street toward Doc McNab's little house. It was a white clapboard house, neat, with a white picket fence. Brock pounded on the door.

A lamp flickered inside. The door opened and Doc stood there, his white hair tousled from sleep, a long white nightshirt covering him, except for hairy, skinny shanks that protruded beneath. Brock said, "Get some pants and your bag. Someone's down in the alley behind the saloon, beaten badly, and I think it's Arnold Means."

Doc turned away from the door, hurrying. He was back in a moment, carrying his bag, wearing

15

shoes and pants into which the nightshirt had been tucked. He followed Brock down the street, half running to keep up with Brock's long strides.

Brock stopped at the saloon. He went in and came out a moment later with a lighted lantern in his hand.

He didn't take time to lock the saloon door again. He hurried on down the street, rounded the corner, and turned into the alley when he came to it.

Doc was half a dozen steps behind. The man lying unconscious in the alley was, indeed, Arnold Means. Doc knelt beside him and felt the pulse in his throat. It was weak and erratic and he said, "It's bad."

"You think he's gonna die?"

Doc did not reply. After several moments of examining Arnold's head, he looked up at Brock and said, "Get some help. Get something to carry him on — a door if you can't find anything else."

"Sure, Doc. Right away." Brock turned and ran.

Arnold groaned. Doc said, "Arnold? Can you hear?"

"Uh-huh." The voice was weak.

"Who did it? Do you know?"

"Marv. . . ."

"Shapiro? You sure?"

"Uh-huh. An' Frank."

"Avila? The one that works for you?"

"Uh-huh." Arnold groaned again.

Doc said, "Arnold, you couldn't be mistaken, could you?"

But Arnold didn't answer him. He had slipped back into unconsciousness. Doc McNab heard running footsteps and turned his head. Matt Wyatt, the sheriff, was hurrying up the alley toward him, unmistakable because of his size and the way he walked. Doc knew there was nothing more he could do for Arnold Means. Not until he got him to where there was some light.

Wyatt didn't ask any foolish questions, but his eyes didn't miss anything. He saw the scuffed tracks in the alley dirt. He saw the torn clothing that had been ripped from Daisy and thrown aside. Then he stood between Doc and the alley mouth and asked, without turning his head, "Did he say anything?"

Doc didn't know why he was so reluctant to repeat what Arnold had said. "A few words. He came to for a minute, maybe."

"What did he say?"

"I don't know. . . ."

"You don't know what he said? Or you don't know if you ought to repeat it to me?"

Doc said resignedly, "I don't have a choice, do I?"

"No."

"He said it was Marv Shapiro. And Frank Avila."

Matt Wyatt did not reply. He stood, legs

spread, waiting. After a little while several men entered the alley, carrying lanterns and a door that had been hastily removed from somewhere. Wyatt took time to light a cigar and to caution the men against messing up the tracks. Then he strode down the alley, heading for Sol Shapiro's house.

CHAPTER

2

The Shapiro house was the largest in the town of Kiowa. It stood at the corner of G Street and Elm, surrounded by cottonwoods grown tall in the ten years since the house had been built. Lilacs in bloom sheltered the porch from the street, their fragrance heavy in the cool night air.

It was a three-story house, its gables ornamented with elaborate scrollwork that in a later age would be called "gingerbread," and it was dark.

Wyatt opened the gate and went up on the porch. He gave the bell a vigorous twist, waited a moment, then gave it another one. Lamplight flickered faintly through the leaded, stained glass in the door, and it finally opened. Sol Shapiro stood there in his nightshirt, a lamp in his hand. He was frowning, and his voice made no effort to conceal his irritability. "What in the hell is the matter with you, waking me up at this time of night?"

"I've got to see Marv, Mr. Shapiro. Right away."

"It'll have to wait until morning." Shapiro closed the door.

Wyatt gave the bell another vigorous twist, and the door was yanked open a second time. He stepped into the house, pushing the banker aside. "I said I wanted to see Marv. I want to see him now."

"You can't . . . !" Shapiro stopped, too sensible a man to argue with something that was already done.

Wyatt said, "Show me his room."

Shapiro shrugged resignedly. "Come on," he said sourly, "I guess you won't be satisfied until I do."

He led the way up the stairs, along a carpeted hall to a room at the end of it. He knocked once, then opened the door and stepped inside. Wyatt followed him.

There was a pile of clothes on the floor beside the bed. Marv made a lumped shape beneath the covers, his back to the door. Wyatt didn't say anything. Neither did Sol.

No movement was apparent in the figure on the bed. Wyatt couldn't even see Marv breathe. He said, "Marv."

The figure stirred, and after a moment turned over. The boy blinked at the lamp and raised both hands to knuckle his eyes. But there was no sleep in them. They were wide awake, not lacking comprehension as they would have been had the boy really been asleep. Wyatt said harshly, "Stand up."

Marv got out of bed. He was in his underwear. There was a long fresh scratch along one side of his face. Wyatt crossed to the bed and picked up the pillow. There was a thin line of blood on the pillowcase, the same length as the scratch.

Stooping, he picked up the trousers on the floor. They were covered with dust and dirt. He tossed them at the boy. "Get dressed and come with me."

Sol Shapiro turned to face Wyatt, his manner protective. "Now wait a minute, Matt. What's he supposed to have done?"

"Daisy Middleton was dragged into the alley a while ago by a bunch of boys. Arnold Means tried to help her, and they beat him up. One of the boys was Marv, and I'm taking him to jail."

Sol swung his head to look at Marv. "Is that true?"

"Naw, it ain't."

"Then how did you get that scratch?"

"I ran through some bushes, comin' home."

Wyatt dumped the pillow out of the pillow-case, then folded the pillowcase and tucked it into his belt. He said, "Get dressed. I haven't got all night."

Sol said, "Matt, wait. Don't put the boy in jail. Maybe what he says is true."

"And maybe it ain't. Come on, kid."

Marv pulled on his pants and shrugged into his shirt, which was torn. He sat down on the bed and pulled on his boots. He got up and looked at Wyatt, cowed now and scared.

21

Sol said, "Can't I bring him in tomorrow?"

Matt Wyatt stubbornly shook his head.

Marv streaked for the door. Wyatt tried to block him, but he was too late. Marv pounded down the stairs, with Wyatt in thunderous pursuit. He reached the front door before Wyatt collared him. He tried briefly to fight, but stopped when Wyatt cuffed him roughly on the side of the head.

The sheriff marched him out before Sol had time to get down the stairs. He heard the banker calling after him, but he didn't stop.

They had gone a block before Marv asked defiantly, "What're you gonna do with me?"

"Put you in jail."

The jail was on Kansas Street, half a block below its intersection with Longhorn, the street on which Daisy lived. Wyatt kept a grip on Marv Shapiro's arm all the way. He didn't want to have to chase the boy again. On open ground, Marv might possibly get away from him.

There were several lights burning in Doc McNab's house. Brock Davidson had reopened the saloon, and several men were standing at the bar. They did not, apparently, see the sheriff and Marv Shapiro pass.

The two reached the jail. The door was unlocked. Wyatt dragged Marv inside. Without lighting a lamp, he took him back to one of the cells, shoved him in, and slammed the door. He locked it and removed the key.

He went back out, still without lighting a

lamp. This time he locked the front door of the jail. He headed down Kansas Street toward the railroad tracks. There were some shacks on the other side of the tracks. Frank Avila lived in one of them with his mother, who took in laundry. Frank sometimes worked for Arnold Means in the hardware store.

Wyatt's eyes were angry as he knocked on the door of the Avila shack. A lamp was lighted almost immediately, and a few moments later Mrs. Avila, wearing a nightgown, opened the door. Wyatt said apologetically, "Good morning, Mrs. Avila. I'm sorry, but I want Frank."

He heard the back door slam and whirled instantly. He was a big man, and slow to get up speed, but once he did, he was faster than Frank Avila. He rounded the corner, charged toward the alley, taking the low rickety fence in stride. He saw Frank pounding down the alley, and swerved to follow him. Behind him he heard Mrs. Avila screeching something at Frank in Spanish, something he didn't understand.

Frank's flight was a confession of guilt, just as Marv Shapiro's had been. As he ran, Wyatt wondered who else had been involved. There had to have been more than two. Two couldn't have beaten Arnold Means and torn the clothes from Daisy at the same time.

At the corner, Frank swerved toward the railroad tracks. Some empty boxcars were on a siding alongside the cattle pens. He ducked behind them, with Wyatt only fifty feet behind. When Wyatt came around the boxcars, Frank was not in sight.

Instantly, Wyatt dropped to his hands and knees, looking beneath the cars. He didn't see anything and, motionless, he didn't hear anything either. Cautiously, he walked along the line of cars. He didn't have his gun, and he hoped Frank didn't have one.

Passing the open door of one of the cars, he glanced toward it. At the same instant, Frank, hiding inside, launched himself.

He struck the sheriff and knocked him sprawling. He had a short length of broken corral pole in his hands, and he struggled to his feet and swung it savagely.

Wyatt caught it on an upraised left forearm, but the club had enough force to instantly numb his arm. Frank took off again, leaving the club behind.

Wyatt pounded after him. This time there was no place for Frank to hide, no place for him to dodge. It was straightaway along the railroad tracks. Wyatt caught him around the waist and brought him down before they had gone a hundred yards. Frank struggled, and Wyatt struck him a heavy-handed blow on the side of the head. Frank stopped struggling.

Angrily, Wyatt dragged him toward the jail. His left arm was still numb from the blow Frank had struck. Reaching the jail, he unlocked it, pushed Frank in, dragged him back to another cell and locked him in.

Returning to the office, he lighted a lamp and carried it back into the corridor between the cells. Both boys sat sullenly on their cots. Frank stared at him. Marv Shapiro looked at the floor between his feet.

Wyatt looked at Frank. "Why? Why Arnold Means?"

Frank did not reply, but neither could he continue to meet the sheriff's eyes. Wyatt turned his head and looked at Marv. "Who else was with you?"

Marv didn't look up, and he didn't speak. Wyatt said, "All right. You two can take the punishment, if that's what you want. Attempted rape. Assault. That'll do for a start."

Marv raised his head. "Attempted rape? Of a whore?"

Wyatt said, "You say that like you thought she was some kind of animal. She's got a right to say no just like any woman has. If you'd gone to her house with a dollar, you wouldn't have had to rip the clothes off her."

Marv said, "Wait until tomorrow. My pa will get me out of here."

Wyatt shrugged. "Maybe. But what about Frank?"

"He'll get Frank out too."

Wyatt turned and went back into the office. He closed the door, leaving the cells in darkness. He blew out the lamp and went into the street. There were a lot of lights on in town by then.

Word of something like this traveled fast, like a prairie fire in a wind.

He passed the saloon without stopping, and went straight to Doc McNab's. He knocked, and Mrs. McNab came to the door. Wyatt took off his hat and went inside. Mrs. McNab, a plump, motherly woman, disappeared. A few moments later, Doc McNab came into the room.

Wyatt asked, "How's Arnold, Doc? Can I talk to him?"

McNab shook his head.

"Why not? Is he still unconscious?"

"He's dead."

The words hit Wyatt like a blow in the stomach. "Dead? How can he be dead?"

His voice trembling with anger, Doc said, "Massive brain hemorrhage. He was kicked to death. But I can't believe those boys. . . ."

"They did it. They both ran when I went after them."

"Did you get them both?"

"They're down in the jail."

"Did they admit it?"

"Not yet. But they will." He was thinking about Arnold Means, lying dead. Because he'd tried to help a woman who needed help. It didn't matter that Daisy probably wouldn't have been hurt, even if he hadn't intervened. It didn't matter that Daisy wasn't worth dying for. Arnold Means had behaved the way a decent man should behave. He had died because he had.

But his death was stupid and senseless and

needn't have happened at all. It had been an act of mob violence by boys who had never done anything violent before. Wyatt knew there had to have been more than two. Two wouldn't have attacked Means so savagely.

He turned and went out, closing the door quietly behind him. He headed for the jail. He intended to get the names of all the boys who had participated in the attack tonight. Because tomorrow all hell was going to break loose in Kiowa.

There was a faint line of gray on the eastern horizon as he headed for the jail. Tomorrow was already here.

CHAPTER

3

Matt Wyatt was a big man, six feet three inches tall. He weighed two hundred and fifteen pounds, and there was no fat on him. He was thirty-two years old, and had been sheriff here for five years, deputy sheriff for three years previous to that. He had come up the trail from Texas eight years ago with a herd of three thousand Texas longhorns, had blown three months' wages in a single night, and had waked up the following day in jail with the king of all headaches, in complete ignorance of where his next meal was coming from. He'd never had a horse of his own, and his saddle was such a wreck, the man in the livery barn wouldn't even buy it from him.

Harry Lomax, the sheriff, had liked his looks. He'd offered him a job as deputy, and Wyatt had grabbed it the way a drowning man grabs a straw. Lomax was killed three years later, shot down in the street by a drunken cowboy he was trying to jail without using his gun. After that, Wyatt had been acting sheriff for a year. When he ran for the office the following year, he was elected overwhelmingly.

Sheriff was for a two-year term. He'd been reelected twice, the second time last November. He was suddenly glad he didn't have to face reelection right away. The way things were going, he would be the most unpopular man in the county by nightfall, if it wasn't sooner than that.

He unlocked the door of the jail and went inside. He closed it and lighted the lamp. He could hear the two boys talking back in the cell block, but he couldn't tell what they were saying, because their voices were muffled by the closed door.

He lighted a cigar and puffed thoughtfully on it for a moment. Then, carrying the lamp, with the cigar clamped between his teeth, he opened the door and went back to talk to them.

They fell silent the minute they heard the door. Wyatt said, "Been talking, boys? Decided what you're going to do?"

For an instant they were silent. Then Marv Shapiro said, "What do you mean, what we're going to do?"

Wyatt said, "About telling me who the others were."

Frank said, "There wasn't no others. And even if there was, we wouldn't snitch on them."

Wyatt puffed his cigar and shrugged. "Up to you, I guess."

Marv said, "My pa will get us out. He'll beat

hell out of me, but he ain't going to let me stay in jail."

Wyatt blew a mouthful of smoke at him. "Your pa won't have much to say about it."

"What are you talking about? Daisy ain't hurt. Nothin' happened to her that hasn't happened a thousand times before."

"Nope. I'm thinking about Arnold Means."

Marv said, "I never touched him. I was busy with Daisy."

Wyatt said, "Don't matter. Rape is a felony, and you were committing a felony. Anybody hurt during the commission of a felony — well, it's everybody's doing."

"How bad is he hurt?"

Wyatt let it drop like a bomb. "Hurt? I thought you knew. He's dead."

There was a silence that was clammy and cold, like water on a stone cellar floor. Marv tried to speak, choked, swallowed, and cleared his throat. Then he tried again. "You're lyin'."

"Nope. I'm not lying." He turned and headed toward the door. "You'll find that out when your pa comes to see you later on. In the meantime, I'd think on it. Course, if you want to take the punishment for all the others that were with you, I guess it's up to you."

He put a hand on the door and opened it. Marv shrieked, "I never touched Mr. Means. I swear to God, I never put a hand on him."

"Makes no difference, Marv. Like I told you, you were committing a felony. So all of you are equally guilty of murder. That's what they'll call it. Murder in the first degree. That means they can hang you for it."

Marv moaned, "Oh God!"

Frank Avila said, "Wait!"

Wyatt looked at him.

"What if we do tell you who the others were?"

Wyatt shrugged. "Not up to me. It's up to the judge when you go to trial. I'll find out whether you tell me or not. Likely Daisy knows."

Frank Avila sounded beat. "All right. I'll tell you. No use in us taking this all alone."

"Who were they?"

"Carl Eggers and Orvie Gunderson."

"That's all?"

"That's all."

"Drinking, were you?"

"Marv stole a bottle of whiskey out of the back room of the saloon. Brock left the door unlocked when he came out to empty a bucket of slop."

"All right boys." Wyatt went back into his office and closed the door. There was no use going after Orvie Gunderson. He was out at the ranch by now, or at least well on his way. His father had a ten thousand acre spread fifteen miles from town.

But he could get Carl Eggers, because Carl lived in town. The thought of having to pick him up made him feel a little sick. Carl was the son of Del Eggers, who worked part time as sheriff's deputy. Del and Wyatt were friends. They liked and understood each other. There was a rare kind of closeness between them that Wyatt had never known with another man except for Sheriff Lomax. Now he had to arrest Eggers' son and throw him into jail. He had to gather evidence that would send him to the gallows. It made him sick to think of it.

This was the dirty part of having the sheriff's job. He muttered savagely, "Damn! Damn it to hell!"

He blew out the lamp and stepped outside. The street was gray with dawn. People were crossing back and forth, more, he thought, than was usual for this time of day.

He carefully locked the door of the jail and pocketed the key. He thought that maybe he ought to have his gun, then discarded the idea. He didn't need a gun to take Carl. And Del Eggers had too much respect for the law to resist him, even when his own son was concerned.

Del Eggers lived with his wife, their son, and daughter, in a modest one-story frame house on B Street, a block east of Doc McNab's. Wyatt walked toward it slowly and reluctantly, hating what he had to do, trying to figure out some way to tell Del that wouldn't hurt so much.

But there wasn't any way. Carl was guilty of murder, and there was no way to sugarcoat the news.

He thought of Carl's mother, a sweet-faced, pleasant woman who kept a spotless house and cooked excellent meals. What the hell made a boy, raised like Carl had been, do a thing like that? Wyatt had no answer. Maybe there wasn't one. Maybe, he thought, there is something savage and murderous in everyone. Maybe in some it comes out. Maybe in others it does not. The rationalizing didn't comfort him, because he knew it was faulty and made no sense. Some people are capable of killing. Some are not. That was the truth. Carl and Marv and Orvie and Frank happened to be four who were capable of it. Four who just happened to be together when the opportunity arose.

Or was he being too harsh on them? Wasn't it possible that Arnold's death had been an accident? Reluctantly he shook his head. No. Doc McNab had said he was literally kicked to death, and Doc hadn't been talking about a kick or two. They had kicked and kicked and kicked in a frenzy until Arnold Means was dead. Maybe they'd have killed Daisy if Arnold hadn't interfered. He didn't think so, but it was possible. For those few minutes, they had been animals, savages out of the beginning of time.

Boys. The youngest fifteen, the oldest seventeen. Boys, maybe, but they had the strength of men. They had killed like men. Now they would have to pay the penalty just like men.

Halfway there, he realized he was deliberately walking slow. He didn't want to face Del Eggers. He didn't want to tell him what his son had done.

He speeded up, walking faster, forcing himself. The sun touched the high clouds and turned them pink. There was a moist, earthy smell in the air, the smell of early morning and early summertime.

The sun's rays were touching the tallest of the trees in town as he knocked at the back door of Del Eggers' house.

Eggers, on the back porch washing, called, "Come on in, Matt."

Matt Wyatt opened the screen door and stepped in onto the porch. He realized that he still had nothing on but pants, into which his nightshirt was tucked, and boots. He had a hat crammed down over his tousled, uncombed hair.

Eggers said, "Come in and have some breakfast." He raised his voice and called, "Emmy! Put on a plate for Matt!"

Wyatt shook his head. "I can't stay. I came for Carl."

"Carl? You got some work for him?"

Wyatt shook his head. Eggers wasn't making this any easier.

Eggers, his face dried, a comb in his hand, finally took a good look at Wyatt's face. He said, "Something's wrong."

Wyatt nodded.

"What is it? Something about Carl?"

Wyatt nodded again. "I've got to arrest him, Del."

"Arrest him? For God's sake why? What did he do?"

Wyatt glanced toward the kitchen door. Del

Eggers said, "She's got a right to hear. Maybe you'd better go on in."

Wyatt went into the kitchen. He could tell immediately that Emily Eggers had already heard. Her face was pale, and her hands, as she set the table, were trembling. Eggers, who had followed him into the kitchen, now repeated, "What did he do?"

"He and three others dragged Daisy Middleton into an alley and ripped the clothes off her. Arnold Means interfered and they beat him. . . ." He couldn't force himself to complete the sentence. Not in front of Emily.

For a long moment, Del Eggers studied Matt Wyatt's face. At last he said, "Could you be mistaken, Matt?"

Wyatt shook his head. "I've got two of them in jail, Marv Shapiro and Frank Avila. They implicated Carl."

"Who was the other one?"

"Orvie Gunderson."

Del nodded. "They run together. The four of them." He was shocked and almost numb. Emily stood beside the stove, twisting her apron between her hands. Her face was stricken, and Matt Wyatt couldn't meet her eyes. Del said, "I'll get him, Matt."

Wyatt nodded. "I'll wait for you outside." He went out onto the porch, crossed to the screen door, and stepped out into the yard. He was going to have to tell Del that Arnold Means was dead. But maybe he could do it so that Emily wouldn't hear. She'd find out eventually, but maybe by the time she did, she'd be better able to withstand the shock.

He heard her weeping now, and he heard Del's angry voice somewhere deep within the house. After about ten minutes Carl came out, followed by his father. He was dressed. He looked sheepish and very scared. Wyatt said, "Come on."

Del said, "I'll go with you."

Wyatt shook his head. "Come down later if you want. Stay with Emily now."

Del nodded, giving Wyatt a grateful glance. Wyatt said, "Come on, Carl."

Carl walked west along Elm Street. For a while he didn't say anything. Passing Doc McNab's, he asked, "Arnold ain't hurt bad, is he Mr. Wyatt?"

Wyatt said brutally, angry and thinking of Del and Emily, "He's dead."

"Dead?" Carl stared at him. Suddenly he whirled and bolted, and Wyatt, who had expected this, pounded after him less than half a dozen feet behind. Carl began to draw away and Wyatt dived for him, encircling his legs with both arms and bringing him crashing to the ground.

Carl sat up and began to fight him. Wyatt released him, seized one of his arms and twisted it behind his back. He raised it until Carl yelled with pain. He didn't want to hit Carl. But he didn't intend to let him get away.

He marched Carl before him all the way to the jail, unlocking it without letting go. He pushed him inside and back through the door leading to the cells. He put him in the cell with Frank Avila, slammed the door, locked it, and pocketed the key.

None of the boys had anything to say. They all looked scared, as if they would have liked to undo what had been done last night. Wyatt said, "I'll get you some breakfast as soon as the restaurant opens up."

He went outside, locking the door behind him. For a moment he stood on the walk in front of the jail, letting the sun soak in. Then he turned and headed for home, a small, one-room house at the corner of Longhorn and G. He went in, got dressed properly, then washed and shaved. He trimmed his wide mustache, which almost hid his mouth, meticulously. He put on a clean white shirt and over it the vest to which was pinned his sheriff's star. He strapped on his cartridge belt and holstered gun.

He went out again and headed for the restaurant. After breakfast he'd have to go after Orvie Gunderson. And he dreaded it.

CHAPTER

4

The restaurant was on Texas Street between B and Kansas Street. Wyatt could smell coffee as soon as he rounded the corner of the Kiowa Hotel. He stepped into the restaurant, crossed to the counter and sat down. Ma Sorenson came from the kitchen, her broad face red and perspiring, wiping her hands on her apron. Wyatt said, "Coffee, Ma. Then fix me a couple of eggs and a slice of ham. While I'm eating, fix me up three trays to take back with me."

"Them boys, huh?"

He nodded.

"Did they really do it?"

"Looks like it."

She got him a cup of coffee and put it down in front of him. "What gets into kids these days?"

Wyatt shrugged and sipped the coffee. Ma didn't expect an answer, and he didn't give her one. After a moment of shaking her head in apparent bewilderment, she disappeared into the kitchen again.

The coffee tasted good. He felt as though he

hadn't slept at all last night. He could hear something sizzling in the kitchen, and soon afterward caught the smell of ham.

After a while Ma came back, bringing him a plate of ham and eggs and a big plate of fresh-baked biscuits to go with it. She refilled his coffee cup.

Wyatt discovered that the events of the past few hours hadn't impaired his appetite. He finished the ham and eggs and four biscuits, then mopped up the plate with a fifth. He drained the coffee cup. Ma brought three trays, stacked up so that he could carry them. He paid her and stuck the check into his vest pocket. Ma held the door for him and he went out.

He hurried toward the jail, avoiding questions thrown at him by passersby, only nodding or answering in monosyllables. He put the trays down on the walk, unlocked the door and stepped inside. He carefully carried the trays back to the cell. The three boys were quiet and subdued. None of them spoke to him or to each other. They were scared, he thought, good and scared, and they had every right to be.

He heard the outside door and went back to the office. Sol Shapiro and his wife stood just inside. Mrs. Shapiro was weeping. Her eyes were red, her face blotchy, as if she had been weeping for a long time. Sol's face was also red, but from anger, not from grief. He said, "I want you should let Marvin go! Right now, I want you should let him go!"

"I can't let him go."

"He has admitted it, then? Is that why you cannot let him go?"

"He admitted attacking Daisy Middleton. And he admitted stealing a bottle of whiskey from the saloon."

"But he did not attack Arnold Means. He had nothing to do with that."

Wyatt said patiently, "Makes no difference whether he did or not. When those four boys pulled Daisy into the alley, they committed a felony."

"A dirty whore!" Shapiro glanced apologetically at his wife, but she did not seem to have heard. Her eyes were glued to the door that led to the cells at the rear of the building.

Wyatt felt anger stir in him. He said, "Wait a minute! Let's don't try putting the blame for this on her! All she was doing was going home. Your son and three of his friends dragged her into an alley and ripped the clothes off of her. Your son was down in the dirt with her while the other three were killing Arnold Means."

Mrs. Shapiro suddenly began to weep hysterically. Sol Shapiro said furiously, "You don't have to be so . . . so. . . . A lady is present."

Wyatt said wearily, "Well, anyway, you can't get him out of jail. You can see the judge about setting bail, but I doubt if he'll agree. This is a capital crime."

"What is that?"

"A crime where someone's killed."

"But you said yourself that he had nothing to do with the death of Arnold Means."

Wyatt's patience was wearing thin. "The law says that when there is a killing during the commission of a felony, then it is murder in the first degree, and all participants are equally guilty, no matter who actually does the killing. Marv may not have touched Arnold Means, but he's just as guilty as those who did."

"That is not right."

"Right or not, it's the law. You want to talk to Marv? If you don't, you'll have to leave. I've got things to do."

Sol Shapiro nodded. "I would like to talk to him." He looked at his wife. "Stay here, Minnie. It will only upset you more to see him in . . . well, to see him back there."

Wyatt opened the door leading to the cells. Sol went through and Wyatt closed the door after him. He took a chair to Mrs. Shapiro and she sat down heavily. She looked up at him, dried her eyes, and asked in her heavily Jewish voice, "Why, Mr. Wyatt? Why did my Marvin do a thing like this?"

Wyatt shook his head helplessly. "I don't know, Mrs. Shapiro. I don't know."

"He has always been such a good boy. Is it something we did wrong?"

He started to say something about bad company, then stopped himself. None of the other boys were any worse than Marv Shapiro was, with the possible exception of Orvie Gunderson.

41

It wasn't a case of bad company. He didn't know what it was. He shook his head helplessly. "You can't blame yourself, Mrs. Shapiro."

"Then who should I blame?"

"Blame Marv, I guess. I don't know who else you ought to blame."

She began to cry again. He could hear Sol Shapiro shouting back in the corridor between the cells, but he couldn't make too much sense out of it, because most of his words were in Yiddish.

Mrs. Shapiro blew her nose, and Sol came through the door from the cells. He glared at Wyatt, then went out the door. Mrs. Shapiro followed him, her eyes downcast.

Wyatt knew he had to get away. He had to go out and get Orvie Gunderson. But he couldn't leave until Del Eggers arrived to look after the jail.

Nervously, he paced back and forth. Half an hour after the Shapiros had left, Mrs. Avila arrived.

She came in, nervous and afraid. Wyatt took a chair to her and she sat down, perching on the edge of it. He asked, "You want to see Frank?"

She shook her head. "I want to talk to you."

He nodded. "All right."

She seemed to grope for words. Finally she asked, "My Frank . . . did he do what they say he did?"

Wyatt said, "It looks like it, Mrs. Avila."

"He has admitted it?"

Wyatt nodded. "And Arnold Means identified him before he died."

She did not weep. She just looked stunned. And beaten. In a whisper she said, "He is all I have."

Wyatt didn't know what to say. He murmured, "I'm sorry, Mrs. Avila."

She didn't seem to hear. She said, "I was proud to have him be friends with the banker's son, and with the son of your deputy, and with the son of Mr. Gunderson. But I am not proud anymore."

Wyatt watched her uncomfortably. Slowly, she got to her feet. "I have work to do." She went to the door and opened it. "If he needs anything, you will let me know?"

He nodded.

"And if he wishes to see me, you will get word to me?"

He nodded again. She went out and the door closed. He watched her walk down the street, shabby and bent, her eyes downcast.

Turning his head, he saw Del Eggers coming along the street. Eggers was walking slowly, as though dreading what lay ahead. Glancing up as he neared the jail, he saw Wyatt watching him. Immediately he straightened and raised his head. He came into the office and closed the door. He glanced toward the door leading to the cells.

Wyatt said, "Del, I. . . ."

Eggers turned his head. He said firmly, "It's

43

all right." But it wasn't all right. There was a stricken, beaten look in Eggers' eyes. He walked to the window and stood there, staring out. After a while, he asked, "Why? That's what I keep asking myself. Why?"

Wyatt said uncomfortably, "I don't know, Del. I honest-to-God don't know. They were drinkin', I guess, and they got all heated up thinking about Daisy. When Arnold interfered. . . ."

"But why would they kill him? Why didn't they just run?"

"I don't think they meant to kill him, Del."

Eggers was silent for a long time. When he spoke, it was thoughtfully, "I remember a lynch mob I saw once, during the war. It was after the Quantrill raid, and they'd caught a rebel spy." He turned his head and looked at Wyatt. "They weren't people anymore, Matt. They turned into animals. They damn near killed him with clubs before they ever got him hanged."

Wyatt didn't say anything. There was nothing he could say. Eggers was right. The four boys had been caught up in a kind of mob frenzy the night before. Del asked, "What am I going to do?"

Wyatt couldn't answer that. He said, "Watch the jail for me. I've got to pick up Orvie Gunderson."

"Watch the jail? With my boy locked up in it? You'd trust me to. . . . ?"

Wyatt said, "You're the only deputy I've got."

44

Eggers turned his face away. With his back to Wyatt he said, "All right. Go ahead. I'll keep an eye on things."

Wyatt got his hat. He selected a rifle from the rack and got some shells for it. He said, "See you later, Del," and went out into the street.

He was glad to get away. Eggers' voice had been all choked up, and he knew there had been tears in Eggers' eyes. To himself, he cursed sourly and bitterly. He had never hated the job of being sheriff before, but he hated it today. He had hated it last night.

He made himself think of Arnold Means. Arnold had lost his wife, and it had hit him harder than Wyatt had ever seen death hit anyone. They must have been very close, he thought, and maybe Arnold, if he'd had the chance, would have chosen death, to remaining alive without his wife.

But that had no bearing on what had happened. That had nothing to do with the fact that he was dead, kicked to death by the scared boys in the jail right now.

He walked through the vacant lot beside the jail to the stable in back. He stroked his gray's neck a moment thoughtfully, then took the halter off and put a bridle on. He threw the saddle blanket on, followed it with the saddle, and cinched it down. He jammed the rifle, which he had leaned against the wall, down into the saddle boot. Outside he mounted, taking the alley to the railroad tracks and following them to

45

the road that led out toward the Gunderson ranch. The same road went by the ranch owned by the two brothers of Arnold Means. He had to stop and tell them about their brother's death. He was sure they had not yet heard, unless some busybody from town had taken it upon himself to ride out there earlier.

He caught himself thinking, as he rode, of Josie Eggers. He'd been going with her for more than six months, and lately he'd been thinking about asking her to marry him. Now he wished he had. He wished he hadn't put it off.

She'd blame him for her brother's plight, even though she knew the fault wasn't his. She'd blame him for putting Carl in jail. She wouldn't be able to help herself.

He'd have to face her this afternoon. He knew it and he dreaded it. He lifted the horse to a steady trot. The Means' ranch was five miles from town, and he hoped he'd be able to reach it before they left the house for the day.

Briefly he thought about the two. They were as different from their brother Arnold as night from day. He had been a town man, who liked his work in the hardware store.

His brothers were cattlemen. Wyatt had heard them say more than once that they didn't understand how Arnold could bear working inside day after day.

He didn't know how the two would react to the news of Arnold's death. What he did know was that they wouldn't accept it philosophically.

CHAPTER

5

It was past eight o'clock when he turned in at the Means brothers' lane. The house, half a mile off the main road, was a two-story frame in which both families lived. Bertram Means was the oldest. He and his wife had one child, a boy. Young David was nine years old.

Lane Means had two, both girls. One was five, the other three. All three children were in the yard when Wyatt rode into it. Bertram's wife was hanging wash on a clothesline stretched between the back porch and a nearby tree. Wyatt touched his hat. "Your husband around, Mrs. Means?"

"Down at the barn, sheriff. What do you want to see him for?"

"How about Lane? Is he at the barn too?"

"They both are. What's this all about?" She was plainly becoming alarmed.

Wyatt dismounted. He asked, "Mind sending Davie after them?"

She called, "David, go get your father and your uncle. Run now."

David streaked for the barn. He came back a

few moments later, followed by his father and uncle. Both men wore puzzled frowns. When they reached him, Wyatt said, "I'm afraid I have bad news. Arnold is dead."

Both men's faces showed their shock. Bertram said, "Dead? How could he be dead? He was all right day before yesterday."

"He wasn't sick. He was killed last night."

"Killed? Arnold? For God's sake, man, who'd want to do a thing like that? Was it robbery?"

Wyatt was getting increasingly uncomfortable because of the presence of the children and Mrs. Means. "It wasn't robbery. Daisy Middleton was attacked by four boys, and Arnold tried to help her. The boys jumped on him and. . . ."

"And what?"

"Kicked him to death."

Mrs. Means said, "Oh, my God!"

After that there was a heavy silence that lasted for what seemed an eternity. At last Bertram said, "Wyatt, if this is some kind of joke, it ain't funny. It ain't funny at all."

Wyatt said, "It's no joke, Mr. Means. I'm sorry, but it's true."

Another silence. Mrs. Means began to cry. She called, "Girls, you come on in the house. You come right now."

They started to argue with her, but her weeping and something about her expression stopped them. Scared and cowed, they went into the house. Mrs. Means followed them. Bertram asked, "Who were the boys? You got them in jail?"

"I've got three of them."

"Who are they?"

"Marv Shapiro. Frank Avila. Carl Eggers."

"Your deputy's boy?"

Wyatt nodded.

"And who's the fourth?"

"Orvie Gunderson. I'm headed out there right now to pick him up."

Both men were silent several moments while digesting this. Both were obviously stunned. At last Lane managed, "Where's Arnold now?"

Wyatt said, "I left him at Doc's. I suppose Doc has had him moved to the undertaker's. If he hasn't, he will."

"Arnold must've lived a while then. If he's at Doc's."

Wyatt nodded. "He was still alive when Brock Davidson found him."

"And he named them boys?"

"Two of them. I got the other two names from them."

Bertram said, "Jesus! Arnold dead! An' helpin' a goddam whore!"

Wyatt said, "I guess any man would've done the same thing. When you hear a woman screaming, you don't stop to ask what business she happens to be in."

Abashed, Bertram said, "I'm sorry. I guess I didn't mean it the way it sounded."

Wyatt said, "I'll be going." He swung to his

horse's back. He hesitated a moment, looking down. At last, almost reluctantly he said, "The law will take care of this. You just leave it up to the law."

Neither man answered him. Riding out, he heard Bertram say, "Lane, go hitch up a team. I reckon we'd best go to town."

He rode on up the lane to the main road. He turned toward Gunderson's. The Means brothers had taken the news well, he thought. But then they hadn't had time to think on it.

Sol Shapiro would do everything he could to get Marv off. So would Olaf Gunderson. And if, by some chance, they did get the two boys off, then the Means brothers would be capable of taking matters into their own hands.

But maybe it wouldn't come to that. Maybe everybody would be content to let the law take its proper course. Maybe. But Wyatt didn't really believe they would.

The sun was warm, and the June sky was dotted with small and puffy clouds. A meadowlark trilled, to be answered by another one. He passed a bunch of cattle grazing near the road, and once he saw an antelope on a hilltop half a mile away. He thought about Josie, and wondered if she had heard about what had happened yet.

Maybe she wouldn't blame him for arresting Carl, he thought. Her father hadn't blamed him, and maybe she wouldn't either. She might understand that he was only doing his job.

50

But he didn't believe it. And if Carl was hanged or sent to prison, how could Josie ever forgive the man who had been responsible? He felt depressed and angry and kicked his horse into a lope.

The Gunderson place was ten miles past the Means' ranch. He reached it about eleven o'clock. The road ended in Gunderson's yard. Beyond, Gunderson's range stretched away to a distant line of rounded hills.

At this time of day, most of Gunderson's hands were away from the house. But someone was shoeing a horse in the blacksmith shop. He could see the smoke from the forge, and he could hear the ring of the hammer against the anvil. He dismounted and went straight to the back door of the house, a big, three-story affair that looked like a twin of the Shapiro house in town.

Mrs. Gunderson came to the door. "Why hello, Mr. Wyatt! Come on in the house. I suppose you want to see Mr. Gunderson."

He nodded, opened the screen door and stepped inside. He took off his hat and stood there, turning it uncomfortably in his hands. Mrs. Gunderson said, "He isn't here right now, but he'll be in for dinner at noon. Won't you stay?"

Wyatt said, "I'd like to, ma'am, but I ought to be getting back."

"Without seeing Mr. Gunderson?"

"Can't you tell me where he is?"

"Jake might know. He's out in the blacksmith shop."

Wyatt nodded and escaped. He hadn't wanted to ask about Orvie, and he didn't want to take Orvie without Olaf Gunderson knowing about it. Gunderson was going to raise enough hell even if things were handled right.

He crossed the yard to the blacksmith shop, a separate building near the barn. Chickens, scratching in the dust, scattered ahead of him. A small herd of weaner pigs were rooting in the shade beside the barn. Wyatt stuck his head into the blacksmith shop. Jake Newcomb had a horse's right hind hoof up between his leather-clad knees, fitting a shoe to it. He glanced up. "Hello, Matt."

"Hello, Jake. Where's your boss?"

"Olaf? Hell, I don't know. Him an' Orvie rode out early this mornin'. Didn't say where they were goin', an' I didn't ask. They'll be in for dinner in a little bit."

He put the horse's hoof down and returned the horseshoe to the forge. He worked the bellows briefly until the shoe glowed red. He took it out with his tongs, laid it on the anvil and shaped it expertly. He quenched it and straightened up. He fished in his pocket for his Bull Durham sack, and offered it to Matt. Wyatt shook his head. Jake rolled a cigarette, stuck it in his mouth and lighted it. "What do you want to see him for?"

Wyatt did not reply. The relaxed atmosphere here told him Orvie had not confessed to anyone. Jake turned, picked up the shoe he had been working on, and once more tried it for fit against the horse's hoof. This time the fit was perfect. He stuck a handful of horseshoe nails in his mouth, picked up a hammer, and began to nail the shoe on, driving in the nails, bending them down and then clipping them off where they emerged from the horse's hoof. He was finished in a few minutes. He clinched the nails and filed them smooth. He released the horse's hoof.

Wyatt, standing outside, saw two men riding in. He instantly recognized one of them as Olaf Gunderson. The man's size was unmistakable.

He was six-feet-two-inches tall and weighed, Wyatt supposed, two hundred and twenty pounds. He had a thick chest, was a little paunchy, and had legs that seemed both too short and spindly to support the weight of his massive head, chest, and arms. He rode into the yard and swung easily to the ground. Orvie, with him, had turned pale. He looked at Wyatt like a scared rabbit, took the reins of his father's horse, and rode into the barn.

Gunderson boomed cordially, "You're just in time for dinner, Wyatt. Let's get washed and go inside."

Wyatt shook his head. "I can't stay. I'm afraid I've got bad news for you."

Olaf, already on his way to the pump, stopped and turned his head. "Bad news?"

"I've come after Orvie, Mr. Gunderson. I've got to take him back to town."

"Why? What for? Did he get drunk and tear something up? Tell me what the damages are and I'll give you the money to take care of it."

Wyatt shook his head. "It's not going to be that easy, Mr. Gunderson." For some reason, Gunderson's unconcern irritated him.

Gunderson frowned. "What are you trying to say, sheriff? Maybe you'd better come right out with it."

Wyatt nodded. "All right. Early this morning Orvie and three others pulled Daisy Middleton into an alley and ripped the clothes off her." He could see a faint grin forming on Olaf Gunderson's heavy face. He said, "Arnold Means heard her screaming, and ran into the alley to help. The boys attacked him and beat him up. Only they didn't stop at that. Arnold Means is dead."

The half smile had disappeared from Olaf's face. He glanced toward the open door of the barn, then back at Wyatt again. For an instant he looked as though he didn't know what to do. Turning his head once more toward the open door of the barn, he bawled, "Orvie! Come here!"

It seemed like a long time before Orvie appeared. When he did, he looked more scared than Wyatt had ever seen him look.

He was a big boy, as tall as his father. He was already top-heavy, the way his father was, but he had neither hardened nor filled out as much. Olaf Gunderson said harshly, "You do what Wyatt says you did?"

Orvie tried to look innocent, but he didn't bring it off. Not convincingly. Olaf said, "Well?"

Orvie said, "I don't know what he says I did."

"He says you an' three others pulled Daisy Middleton into the alley an' ripped the clothes off her. He says Arnold Means interfered, and the four of you beat him to death."

Orvie swallowed, then said thinly, "He's a liar, Pa. I swear to God. . . ."

Wyatt said, "Get your horse, Orvie. I've got to take you into town."

Orvie looked helplessly at his father, and Olaf said, "Wait a minute now! Just wait a minute now! You can't haul this boy off to jail just on your own say-so."

Wyatt said, "It's not my say-so. The other three boys have confessed. They've implicated Orvie, and all three of them are in jail."

Gunderson looked at his son again. Wyatt could tell by his expression that he knew the charge was true. Orvie was guilty. His face gave him away. Gunderson said, "You ride out, Orvie. You get out of here until the sheriff's gone. I'll talk to you when you get back."

Wyatt said, "Damn it, Olaf, don't make this any harder than it already is."

Orvie had already ducked back inside the barn. Wyatt, drawing his gun, started after him.

He heard Olaf coming behind him. He hadn't expected it, and he only had time to turn his head. Then Olaf's great body hit him from behind, slamming him forward and throwing him to the ground.

Wyatt was startled, but he wasn't stunned. And he had the gun in his hand. Olaf came clawing after him, and he swung it at the big man's head, more out of reflex than anything. It struck, drawing instant blood from Olaf's ear, but not even stunning him.

Olaf let out a roar that was like the roar of an angry bull. Wyatt struck again, this time with all his strength. The gun barrel hit Olaf on the top of the head, with a crack that must have been audible all the way to the house. This time the big man slumped.

Wyatt rolled his heavy body aside and struggled to his feet. He pointed the gun at Jake. "You're not going to do anything foolish, are you?"

Jake shook his head. Wyatt said, "Hitch up a buggy and help me throw him into it."

"What are you going to do?"

Turning his head, Wyatt could see Orvie, already a quarter-mile away and riding hard. He said, "I'm going to put him in jail."

Jake disappeared into the barn. Mrs. Gunderson came out of the house. Her face was white and scared.

Wyatt said, "You'd just as well know, Mrs. Gunderson. Orvie and some other boys killed a man last night. Your husband wouldn't let me take him, so I'm taking your husband instead."

She didn't speak. She licked her lips and

wiped her hands on her apron. Jake drove a buggy out of the barn. Wyatt holstered his gun and helped Jake lift Gunderson into the buggy. He got his horse and tied him on behind. He mounted to the buggy seat and drove the rig out of the yard. Jake and Mrs. Gunderson stood looking helplessly after him.

CHAPTER

6

Mrs. Shapiro wept softly all the way home. The sounds only increased Sol's irritability. He had no time to show sympathy for her. His mind was too busy trying to think of some way he could get Marvin out of this terrible predicament. He didn't even think of Arnold Means. Nor did he think of Daisy Middleton.

He walked all the way home with his wife. He went inside and, despite the early hour, got a bottle of homemade wine. He gulped a glass, then gulped a second one, something he had never done before. Wine was to be enjoyed, by slow sipping, not by gulping the way a thirsty man gulps water.

He left without saying anything to Minnie. He walked swiftly along the street. It wasn't yet time to open the bank. He'd had no breakfast, but he didn't even think of it. Martin Diggs would be in his office over the bank. He was there by seven-thirty every day.

He climbed the steps, his shoulders slumped with discouragement. He still could not believe that Marv had participated in such an attack. It was those other boys, he thought. It had to be the influence of those other boys.

He opened the door at the top of the stairs, went down a short hallway, and entered an office that fronted on the street and had the name "Martin Diggs" and "Attorney at Law" lettered on the door.

Diggs was a grizzled, stocky man, with a head that seemed too large for the rest of him. His office was as untidy as was the man himself. Papers were piled high on his desk. The spittoon beside it had probably not been emptied for a month. There was an odor of stale cigar smoke in the place, and an untidy litter on the floor.

Diggs was a bachelor and had a room at the hotel, which probably explained why he came to his office so early every day. He glanced up, saw Shapiro, and said, "Sit down, Sol. I've been expecting you."

"You've heard, then?"

Diggs nodded. "I've heard."

There was a long silence. At last Sol said, "I've been telling myself all the obvious things — that he's been raised in a good Jewish home, that he's been taught all the things that should be taught to a growing boy. He has worked around the house, and he has helped out at the bank. What makes a boy like that do what he has done?"

"You're sure he did it?"

"He has confessed to it. Except that he says he did not help to beat Arnold Means."

"But he admits the attack on Daisy Middleton?"

Sol nodded unhappily. "The sheriff tells me that makes him just as guilty of murder as the other boys. Is that right, Mr. Diggs?"

Diggs nodded. "Technically it does. Only in practice it don't always work that way."

"What do you mean?"

Diggs studied him, a practical expression in his eyes. "Are you asking me to represent your son?"

"Yes, yes. Of course I am. Why else would I have come here, Mr. Diggs?"

"All right then. We'll get Marv tried separately, not with the other boys. We'll make a big thing out of the fact that Marv never laid a hand on Arnold Means."

"But if the law says. . . ."

Diggs interrupted. "Juries don't always pay strict attention to the law. We got a nice, good-looking, hardworking Jewish boy here, who tried to get himself a whore. Men understand a thing like that. There's damn few of us who can't remember when . . . well, anyway, there'll be a lot of sympathy for him. And if we can get Daisy Middleton to swear Marv was busy with her, while Arnold Means was getting beat — well, I'd say we had a chance."

"You think I ought to go see Daisy Middleton?"

Diggs shook his head. "You leave that up to me."

Shapiro looked relieved. "What do you want I should do?"

"Nothing. Go home. Don't talk to anybody about this thing."

Shapiro nodded. He put on his hat. "You will see Daisy Middleton right away?"

Diggs nodded. Shapiro reached the door and opened it. Diggs said, "Might be that a woman like Daisy would need a few dollars to tide her over until this thing is over with. Might be she'd want to leave town after the trial and make a new start someplace else. You prepared to help her out?"

Shapiro said, "How much?"

"How much is your son's life worth?"

Shapiro frowned before he said, "Yes, yes. Whatever is necessary. Whatever is necessary."

"And my fee might come pretty high."

Shapiro started to ask how much, then closed his mouth. He shut the door, went down the hall, and stepped out onto the landing. Diggs was the only lawyer in town. People knew him and respected him. If he went to another town for another, cheaper lawyer, it wouldn't set well with the local people from whom the jury would be selected. He unlocked the door of the bank and went inside. He locked the door behind him, leaving the shade down over the window glass. He went into his office and sat down. Glumly he stared at the wall beyond his desk, seeing nothing, numb with the shock of what had happened so unexpectedly.

Marvin had done wrong, but Marvin had not participated in beating Arnold Means to death. For that he was deeply grateful. The law might say Marv was guilty, but the fact remained that he hadn't laid a hand on Arnold Means.

Diggs left the office almost immediately after Shapiro did. He heard the door of the bank close and knew Shapiro had gone inside. He descended the stairs, cut across the street diagonally, then walked along Texas Street to F. He walked the block down F Street, then cut across diagonally again to Daisy Middleton's little house. He opened the sagging picket gate and walked up the path through the untended yard to the door. He knocked.

He saw, out of the corner of an eye, the curtain pulled aside slightly from one of the windows. A moment later the door opened, and Daisy stood framed in it.

Diggs said, "I'd like to talk to you."

"Well I don't want to talk to you. Don't you think a girl ever needs to sleep?"

He could tell that she had been drinking. Her speech was slurred, and she swayed slightly in the doorway. One of her eyes was almost black, and her lips were puffy. Her hair was tangled and uncombed. Diggs felt a brief moment of compassion for her. She couldn't be much older than twenty-five. In another five years she'd have difficulty finding a man who would pay a dollar to go to bed with her. Diggs said persuasively,

"There might be some money in it for you, Daisy. That thing in the alley last night might turn out to be the best trick you ever turned."

She stared at him suspiciously. Diggs said, "Just let me come in and talk to you for a minute."

"I ain't goin' to lie."

"Nobody's asking you to lie. Can I come in?"

She nodded grudgingly and stood aside. Diggs opened the screen door and stepped into the house.

It smelled of strong perfume, the way Daisy did. She had on a wrapper and, he supposed, precious little under it. He said, "I'm representing Marvin Shapiro, Daisy. His father hired me."

"What do you want to see me about?"

He studied her face, the black eye and bruised mouth. "Who did that to you? Which one of them?"

"How should I know?" she said sullenly. "It was dark, and the little bastards was all over me."

"At first, you mean?"

"That's what I mean. At first."

"And then Arnold Means heard your screams and came into the alley. Did he yell at them to stop?"

"He sure did. He yelled at them to get away from me."

"And did they?"

"Three of them did. That Jewish boy, though,

he only had one thing on *his* mind. He yelled at the others to get Mr. Means out of there."

"Marv Shapiro?"

"I guess that's his name. Mr. Means called him Marv." She made a weary smile. "I don't usually learn their names until they're old enough to come into the saloon."

Diggs smiled back at her, reassuringly. "And he never stopped — attacking you, I mean."

"No, sir. He kept trying to tear the clothes off me, the little son-of-a-bitch. Does he think I get my clothes for free?"

"Mr. Shapiro is prepared to compensate you for your loss." He watched her reaction carefully. There was the briefest kind of gleam in her eyes, and then it was gone again. Diggs said, "All you have to do is tell the truth. Mr. Shapiro is prepared to be very generous. Generous enough to enable you to go to some other town when this is all over, and make a fresh new start."

She glanced at him cynically, "I'd as soon his generosity came before the trial, not after it, if you know what I mean."

Diggs smiled at her. "You can count on it, Daisy. You won't mind if I prepare a little statement for you to sign, will you?"

She had sobered remarkably in the last few minutes. She said now, "Not so long as some of Mr. Shapiro's generosity comes along with it."

"It will, Daisy. It will." He went to the door. He knew he had better get her to sign a statement before Gunderson got to her. Gunderson would both bribe and threaten her, and there was no telling what a combination of greed and fear might cause her to say. Turning just outside the door, he said, "I'll be back in half an hour, Daisy, and I'll bring the money along with me."

She nodded. He went down the path and through the gate, without hearing the door close behind him, but he did not look back.

He went straight to the bank and knocked. Shapiro let him in. Diggs said, "I want a hundred dollars in gold for Daisy, now. She's agreed to sign a statement. I want to give her another four hundred on the day of the trial. Is that all right?"

"She said Marv had nothing to do with beating Arnold Means?"

"That's what she says. He was busy ripping the clothes off her, she says. Better add twenty to that hundred, so she can buy herself some clothes."

Shapiro started to say something, then changed his mind. There was the ghost of a smile on Diggs' mouth as Shapiro went back to the safe at the rear of the bank.

He returned in a few minutes and dropped six double eagles into the lawyer's hand. Diggs went out, closing the door softly behind him, grinning widely now. He climbed the stairs, and in long-hand wrote out a statement for Daisy Middleton to sign. Then he went back to her house.

She was waiting for him at the door. He went in and handed the money to her. He took the prepared statement out of his pocket. "Can you read, Daisy?"

"No, sir." She flushed faintly.

"Can you sign your name?"

"Yes, sir. I can do that all right."

"Then I'll read the statement to you, and you can sign it when I'm through." The statement was brief and to the point. It said: "On the morning of June 10th, 1877, at about one o'clock, I was attacked by four boys, and pulled into an alley behind the Ace High Saloon. I couldn't identify the boys. When Arnold Means came into the alley to help me, in response to my screams, three of the boys left me and started beating him. The other one, the one they called Marv, yelled at them to get Mr. Means out of there. He kept trying to rip the clothes off me. Then they all got scared and ran. The one called Marv never touched Arnold Means. He was struggling with me all the time."

Diggs asked, "That sound like a true statement of what happened with regard to Marv Shapiro, Daisy?"

"Yes, sir."

"Then sign it. Right here." He showed her where to sign, and she laboriously scrawled her name. He said, "Daisy, on the day of the trial, Mr. Shapiro is going to give you four hundred dollars more. That will buy you some new clothes, get you to another town, and leave you enough to live on until you get yourself a job you like. All right?"

"All right." She hesitated a moment. "I ain't doin' nothing wrong, am I Mr. Diggs?"

"No, Daisy. You're not doing anything wrong. You're only telling the truth. Mr. Shapiro isn't bribing you. He's only trying to make it up to you for what his son did to you last night."

She nodded. The six double eagles were clutched so tightly in her hand that her knuckles showed white.

He went out, and this time heard the door close behind him. Halfway across the street, he thought he heard hysterical laughter behind him, muffled by the walls of Daisy's house.

Chapter

7

Gunderson didn't stir all the way to town, and Wyatt paid little attention to him. He was angry because Gunderson had prevented him from capturing Orvie. He was irritated because now he would have to go back out to the Gunderson ranch after the boy. He was worried because of what Gunderson's crew might do when they heard, from Jake and from Mrs. Gunderson, that the rancher had been knocked out and carted off to jail.

He didn't want Gunderson in jail, even though he had ample cause to charge him with things like obstructing an officer, aiding and abetting a fugitive, and even assault. He wanted Orvie. This business was ugly enough without having it turned uglier.

Now he glanced at Gunderson, having detected, perhaps, a change in the man's breathing. Gunderson did not appear to have stirred. He still lay in the same position. He was still unconscious, or appeared to be.

Half a mile from town, Gunderson moved. He

moved so fast, and so unexpectedly, that he took Wyatt completely by surprise. He flung himself at Wyatt with enough force to roll the two of them clear out of the buggy and onto the dusty road.

The buggy horse stopped immediately. Wyatt's horse, behind, pulled back nervously to the end of his reins, which were tied to the buggy.

Wyatt hit the road on his back, with enough force to knock the breath out of him. He grabbed for his gun, only to discover it had dropped from its holster in the fall. Gunderson saw it, though, and clawed toward it. Reaching it, he seized it and turned, slashing at Wyatt with it. The barrel raked his cheek and nose, drawing blood. He reared back to escape a second blow, but he was too late. The muzzle descended, struck him squarely on the top of the head, and knocked him cold.

Gunderson struggled to his feet. He was angry too, angry at the way Wyatt had manhandled him, angry at the indignity of being carted away from his ranch like so much carrion. He was angry because both Jake and his wife had witnessed his humiliation, and because Orvie might have seen it too.

But mostly, he was angry because he was desperate and didn't know what to do. Orvie was in trouble, the worst trouble of his life. If something wasn't done, and quickly, Orvie was going to hang.

The worst of it was, he believed in Orvie's guilt. He knew what an awful temper Orvie had. It was even worse than his own, which was considerable. He had seen Orvie, on a number of occasions, beating a horse mercilessly, almost frenziedly, because the animal hadn't done exactly what he wanted it to do. He had always stopped the boy. But last night he hadn't been there to stop him. Last night others had been with Orvie, others who had joined in. The result was that Arnold Means was dead.

Gunderson reminded himself that he was used to the feel of power. He knew the power his wealth gave to him. He wasn't used to defeat.

And Orvie was his son. His only son. His only hope for immortality. He and his wife had tried for years to have more children, and they hadn't been able to. He wasn't going to stand helplessly by and watch Orvie convicted of this crime. He wasn't going to let Orvie hang. There had to be some way of getting him out of it. If there wasn't, he'd simply see to it that Orvie got away. There were places the boy could go. He was almost grown, and he'd soon be on his own anyway.

He untied Wyatt's horse from behind the buggy, walked to the edge of the road and tied him to a clump of brush. The sheriff still lay where he had fallen, blood on his nose and cheek, blood trickling from the wound on the top of his head. If he didn't regain consciousness right away, someone was sure to come this way and find him lying here. His own crew would probably be coming into town very soon. They'd pick Wyatt up and bring him in. If he needed the attentions of Doc McNab, they'd see that he got to McNab's house all right.

He climbed into the buggy and clucked at the buggy horse. The animal moved on at a walk. Gunderson slapped his back with the reins, and the horse broke into a trot.

Wyatt had three of the boys in jail. There would be a deputy guarding it, and it wasn't likely he'd get anything out of them that would help Orvie anyway. Arnold Means was dead. But Daisy Middleton was alive. She was the one who could put the noose around Orvie's neck. Or could save him if she wanted to.

He drove the buggy across the railroad tracks, up Kansas Street, and turned left on Longhorn Street. He made another left turn at the next corner and drew the buggy to a halt. He got down, clipped the tether weight to the horse's bridle, and went up the weed-grown walk.

He knocked lightly on Daisy's door. He heard no sound inside, and wondered if she had already gone to work at the Ace High Saloon. He doubted it. She was probably sleeping. After what had happened last night, she had probably had several drinks. She was probably asleep.

He knocked harder, and still got no reply. Exasperated, he pounded thunderously on the door.

He heard Daisy's plaintive, protesting cry

from within the house, coming nearer to the door, complaining irritably all the while. The door opened, and Daisy stood framed in it, clad in a wrapper, her hair tousled, her eyes bleary from sleep and from the liquor she had drunk. He could smell her cheap perfume, and he could smell liquor on her breath.

He pushed past her and went inside. She turned to face him, closing the door behind her. "What makes you think you can come barging in here as if you owned the place?"

"I want to talk to you."

"Oh. You want to talk to me. What am I supposed to do? Fall down on my knees?"

"Don't get smart with me." He realized instantly that he had better not make her mad. It wasn't his way to be diplomatic, but he had better try. He said, "The sheriff was just out at my place. He wanted to arrest Orvie."

She said nothing, but her eyes had sharpened, and some of the sleepiness had gone out of them. Gunderson said, "What happened last night anyway? Would you mind telling me?"

She shrugged. "I was walking home. It was about one o'clock. Brock hadn't closed yet, but there was only Arnold Means in the place, and I was tired."

"And the boys jumped you?"

She nodded. "They came out of the alley. They grabbed me and started pawing me. One of them told one of the others that they'd better drag me back into the alley, unless they wanted the whole damn town to see. He called him Orvie."

Gunderson tried to think of any other Orvies in town, or the surrounding country. He could not. He said, "Go on."

"Well, they threw me down on the ground. They ripped my clothes off, and they hit me several times." She glanced at the floor. "It ain't no secret what I do for a living. But clothes cost money, Mr. Gunderson. I didn't see why they had to rip them off of me. Or why they had to beat me up. Hell, I'd have given them what they wanted."

He was surprised to realize that he felt sorry for the girl. He said, "And so you screamed?"

"Sure I did. Any woman would. Even one like me."

"And Arnold Means came to help?"

"Sure. He yelled at them to get away from me and leave me alone. Then he came running into the alley. All but one of them left me and lit into him. I didn't see everything that happened, because I was fighting the one who'd stayed with me."

"Who was he? Do you know?"

"Marv Shapiro. That's who he was. It wasn't your boy, Mr. Gunderson."

"How do you know it was Marv?"

"He was practically on top of me. He told the other three to get that, excuse me, son-of-a-bitch out of there. Then I heard Mr. Means say, 'Marv? Is that you?' I guess Mr. Means recognized his voice."

"What happened then?"

"All of them but Marv started hitting Mr. Means. I guess they got him down in the alley. I guess they kicked him, because Doc McNab said he was just kicked to death."

Gunderson felt a little sick. In his mind he could see Orvie, beating on a horse, beating savagely, frenziedly. He must have kicked Arnold Means that way.

He groped for the right words. He knew what he wanted to say, and he knew it was callous, but he didn't want it to sound that way. At last he said, "Daisy, Arnold Means is dead."

"I know that," she said.

"Hanging all those boys isn't going to bring him back."

"Maybe they won't hang them, Mr. Gunderson. They're only boys."

"Maybe not, but I can't afford to take the chance. Orvie is the biggest, so he'll get most of the blame."

She didn't say anything. She was watching him closely, suspecting what he was leading up to, but not yet absolutely sure.

Gunderson said, "I'm sure they didn't intend to kill Arnold Means, or even to hurt him. They just lost their heads."

"Yes, sir." She was sure, now, what he was leading up to. The same thing Mr. Diggs had worked up to so carefully.

He said, "Daisy, Orvie's got his faults, plenty

74

of them, but he's all I've got. He's my only son, and I'll never have any more."

She didn't answer that. He said, "Suppose you were to say that two of the boys were attacking you while Arnold Means was getting beat?"

"I couldn't do that, Mr. Gunderson. It just ain't true. I ain't going to lie."

Gunderson asked, "How much do you make, working at the saloon?"

Daisy frowned. She said, "Forty dollars a month, maybe."

"How would you like to have a hundred dollars a month for the rest of your life?"

She stared at him unbelievingly. "Just for saying Orvie was down on the ground with Marv Shapiro an' me?"

"Just for saying that."

For a moment, Daisy was too numb to think. Then she thought about Frank Avila and Carl Eggers. If she lied and got both Marv and Orvie off the hook, Frank and Carl would take the punishment for all four. They would either hang or go to prison for the rest of their lives.

The trouble was, she felt in her heart that Orvie Gunderson was probably the one who had actually killed Arnold Means. There was no way to know for sure, but she, like Olaf Gunderson, had once seen the way his son Orvie beat a horse when he lost his temper over the animal's failure to obey. Carl and Frank, on the other hand, had always seemed to her to be normally decent boys.

Gunderson said, "A hundred dollars a month for the rest of your life. You wouldn't have to work in a saloon anymore." He stared at her and said brutally, "You ain't getting any younger, Daisy. How many more years do you think you've got? Five? Ten?"

Anger flared in her. Not only because of what he had just said, but also because her conviction was growing that if she got Orvie off by lying she would be helping the real killer to escape the consequences of what he had done. Besides insuring the conviction of Frank and Carl, who, while guilty of attacking Means, were probably innocent of killing him.

She had accepted Diggs' offer earlier, because he had not required that she lie. This was different. She shook her head. "I can't do it, Mr. Gunderson. I can't lie, for you or for anybody else."

He scowled, and his eyes turned hard. He said, "You're full of righteousness, aren't you, for a lousy whore? You'll sell yourself to any bastard that has a dollar, but you won't tell a lie!"

Daisy said, "You get out of here, Mr. Gunderson. You get out, or I'll tell the sheriff you threatened me."

He said, less angrily, "What do you want? More?"

"No, sir. I don't want more. I just don't want to tell no lies. I think Orvie was the one, myself. I've seen the way he beats a horse. I think he lost his head and kicked Mr. Means to death, just

76

like he was beatin' on a horse."

Gunderson stared malevolently at her. The situation was so ludicrous, he had an almost irresistible compulsion to laugh. Here was a common prostitute stubbornly insisting that she wouldn't tell a lie. She'd do anything else, but she wouldn't tell a lie.

His face was ugly now. He said, "All right, I've offered you money and the offer stands. But don't you say no to me. You either say what I told you to, or I'll see to it you get beat so bad you'll never work in any damn saloon again. If you live through it, that is. Your teeth will be knocked out, and your nose broken, and there'll be scars all over your face. You've seen Orvie work on a horse, you say. By the time I get through with you, you'll be envying that horse."

He turned, went out the door, and slammed it savagely behind him. As he turned, he had one glimpse of Daisy's white face and wide, terrified eyes. Tramping furiously down the path toward his buggy, he thought, "She'll do it. I don't have to worry about it anymore."

He saw Wyatt coming on his horse. He stood beside the buggy, waiting. He had accomplished his purpose. It didn't matter, now, whether Wyatt threw him into jail or not.

CHAPTER

8

Matt Wyatt came to, lying in the dusty road. There was dried blood on his cheek from the slashing blow struck by Olaf Gunderson. There was a knot on his head as big as a walnut, and there was dried blood in his hair. His head ached ferociously, and he was furious because it was obvious that Gunderson had regained consciousness a long time before he had attacked him, and had lain in the buggy playing possum until he felt strong enough. Then, without warning, he had attacked.

Grumbling because he had not been on guard against such a move, Wyatt struggled to his feet, staggering with dizziness and wincing from the excruciating pain inside his head. He picked up his gun and halfheartedly brushed the dirt from his clothes.

His horse was tied beside the road. He stumbled to the animal, untied him, and with an effort, swung to the saddle and settled himself in it like a lump of clay.

He pointed the horse toward town, his mind

puzzling. Why had Gunderson wanted to get away so badly? Why had he been willing to attack the sheriff for a few minutes' freedom? To return to the ranch? No. The tracks of the buggy were plain in the dusty road heading toward town.

Had he escaped simply because he was angry at the way the sheriff had manhandled him? That seemed doubtful. Gunderson was proud, but he was not a fool.

The only remaining reason had to be that Gunderson wanted to question the witnesses. And since Arnold Means was dead, that meant Daisy Middleton. And, perhaps, Doc McNab.

He kicked his horse into a trot, but he couldn't stand the jolting gait. It made his head ache too ferociously. Squinting against the glare, wincing against the pain, he drew the horse back to a walk.

This way he entered town, crossed the railroad tracks, and angled across several vacant lots below the jail toward Daisy's house. The buggy was standing in front of it, a tether weight clipped to the horse's bridle. While he was still fifty yards away he saw Gunderson come out and walk toward it.

Gunderson saw him and stopped. Wyatt put a hand on the grip of his revolver. He said, "My head aches like hell, and I'm mad as a teased rattlesnake. If you still want to play games, I'm ready for it."

Gunderson didn't say anything. There was a look of satisfaction on his face. Wyatt asked,

"You got a gun?"

Gunderson shook his head. Wyatt said, "You look like the cat that swallowed the canary. What did you get her to say?"

"I didn't get her to say anything. I just asked her what had happened, that's all."

"Yeah. I'll bet you did. Get up in the buggy and drive to the jail. I'll be right behind. Don't try anything, because I've taken all I'm going to take from you."

He glanced at the house. He would have liked to talk to Daisy, but he hadn't time right now. He wanted to know what Gunderson had said to her, and what kind of agreement, if any, they had reached, but it would have to wait.

He followed the buggy to the jail. Gunderson got down, clipped on the tether weight, and then meekly stood waiting for him in front of the jail door. Wyatt dismounted, tied his horse, then said, "Go on in."

"You can't keep me locked up long."

"I can keep you until I get Orvie in custody. Go on in."

Gunderson went in. Del Eggers got up from behind the desk, and Wyatt said, "Search him and lock him up." He took off his hat and sailed it at the desk. Eggers stared at him with concern. "What happened to you?"

"Gunderson. He slugged me with a gun."

"You look like hell. You ought to see the Doc."

"Later."

Eggers said, "Put your hands against the wall, Mr. Gunderson."

Gunderson obeyed. Wyatt watched carefully. He didn't expect any further resistance from Gunderson, but then he hadn't expected any earlier. Del found nothing but a pocketknife. He opened the door and followed Gunderson back to the cells. Wyatt heard one of the iron doors open, then heard it clang shut again. He heard the distinctive noise the key made turning in the lock. Del returned and closed the door. Wyatt said, "Keep an eye on things until I get back."

"You going to see the Doc?"

"Not right now, but I won't be long." He went out. He didn't bother with his horse, but walked around the jail and headed across a vacant lot toward Daisy's house. Passing the barred cell windows, he heard Olaf Gunderson's deep, heavy voice.

He paid no attention, not bothering to stop and listen to what Gunderson had to say. He reached Daisy's house and knocked on the door. Inside, he heard her complaining about nobody letting her get any sleep. The door opened.

Wyatt said, "Daisy, I want you to come down to the jail and make a statement."

"Right now?" she asked incredulously. "Do you know how much sleep I've had?"

He frowned. He had the feeling Gunderson had tried to influence her, and it was probable that Shapiro had also. But Mrs. Avila wouldn't think of it, and Del Eggers hadn't had the oppor-

81

tunity, even if he was unprincipled enough, which Wyatt doubted. He shook his head. "No. Get some sleep. Come in when you wake up."

She didn't close the door. "What kind of statement you want me to make?"

"Just what happened last night."

"And you want me to sign it?"

He nodded. "Any reason why you can't?"

She shook her head, too quickly he thought. "No. Why should there be?"

"I don't know, Daisy. I was just asking. But you think about it. Making false statement is perjury. You can go to jail for it. When you make your statement, be sure it's absolutely true."

She had flushed a little. "Are you trying to say I'd lie?"

"No. But Gunderson wants you to, doesn't he?"

She couldn't meet his eyes.

"And Shapiro got his two cents' worth in too, didn't he?"

"Mr. Diggs was here. But I suppose you already know he was."

He said, "Get your sleep. I'll see you later at the jail."

The door closed. Staggering slightly, Wyatt crossed the street and headed back toward the jail.

Sol Shapiro stayed in his office at the bank all morning. He couldn't face the questions he knew everyone would ask of him. Nor could he face their stares, the way they'd look at him, the way they'd whisper back and forth afterward.

Sol was scared. Marv was his only child, and like Gunderson, he hadn't been able to have any more. He had plans for Marv. He intended to send him East as soon as he was old enough, to the university. When he got back after graduation, he would go into the bank. Eventually the bank would belong to him, and to his sons after him.

But, if Marv was sent to prison, all those dreams would go up in smoke. Bankers with prison records don't generate much public confidence. Nor was there any assurance Marv would get off with a prison sentence. He might be hanged. Even with Daisy's testimony, he might. Nobody knew exactly what had happened in that deserted alley last night. The jury might convict all four of the boys. Arnold Means had two brothers, and he had literally hundreds of friends.

Shapiro got up and began to pace back and forth. Doc McNab had told the sheriff that Arnold Means was literally kicked to death. But what if he were to change that story? What if he were to say Means' death was due to an accidental fall?

His pacing quickened. The mortgage on Doc's house came due in three months. Normally, renewal would be automatic. Doc was frequently late with his payments, but he was not in arrears.

But suppose he refused to renew? There wasn't another bank for a hundred miles. And no bank would lend money in a town that far away when the local bank refused.

Making up his mind suddenly, he put on his hat and left his office. He strode through the thin crowd in the bank lobby, neither looking at anyone nor speaking. He went out, slamming the door, and walked up the street toward Doc's house at the other end of the block.

He reached Doc's house, opened the picket gate, went up the walk and knocked on the door. Doc's wife answered. Shapiro said, "I've got to talk to Doc, Mrs. McNab. Is he here?"

"Yes. Come in, Mr. Shapiro."

Shapiro went in. Mrs. McNab led him across the parlor, opened a door and told him to go in. She closed the door behind him.

The room was Doc's office. Doc was sitting at his desk. He turned, peering nearsightedly through his glasses. Shapiro said, "I've got to talk to you."

Doc got up. "All right, Mr. Shapiro."

"It's about Marv. You know what happened last night, and you know he's in jail."

Doc nodded. "I know."

Shapiro hesitated. At last he said, "I'm not making excuses for him, Doctor. What he did was wrong. But he never touched Arnold Means. He was down on the ground trying to . . . well, you know. He was with Daisy all the time."

Doc asked bluntly, "What has that got to do with me?"

84

"The sheriff says you told him Arnold was kicked to death."

"That's what I told him. Yes."

"Well, what I'm trying to say is, the law says that the boys were committing a felony by attacking Daisy Middleton. It also says that whoever is along when a felony is committed is equally guilty of murder when somebody gets killed."

"I know."

"Well that isn't right, Doctor. Marvin never touched that man, and it isn't right he should get himself hanged for killing him."

Doc McNab said, "I know how you feel, Mr. Shapiro, and I sympathize. But what has all this got to do with me?"

"What if Arnold Means' death was an accident? It would make all the difference in the world. Marvin's going to have to go to jail. I'm resigned to that. But he wouldn't hang! And he wouldn't go to prison for his whole life!"

"But it wasn't an accident. Unless by an accident you mean that the boys didn't actually intend to kill him."

"But what if you was to say it was?"

"You mean lie? You mean perjure myself?"

"It wouldn't be exactly perjury, Doc. And you'd be saving a good boy's life."

Doc shook his head. "That's not my decision to make, Mr. Shapiro. That decision is up to the court."

"But you can make it. You can make it now.

All you have to do is say that Arnold could have died from an accidental fall, that he could have hit his head on a rock. All you got to say is that he *could* have. You don't have to say he did. Anyway, how do you know that the blow that caused his death didn't result from a fall?"

Stubbornly, Doc shook his head.

"You won't do it? Not even when I'm begging you?"

"I can't, Mr. Shapiro. I can't lie under oath."

Shapiro was trembling. He stared at Doc, wondering why he suddenly disliked him so. He hadn't realized until now that Doc hated him, hated Marv, hated Mrs. Shapiro too. Doc hated Jews. That had to be the reason he was doing this. He said, "I wasn't going to say this to you. I thought you was a decent man. But since you won't, I got to remind you. The mortgage on your house is due in less than ninety days. I'm not going to renew it for you, Doctor McNab. Not unless you do what I have asked you to."

"Then I'll get the money someplace else."

"All right. You do that, Doctor McNab. You go to the bank in Hays, and you see what they say when you tell them I have refused to renew. You go to Mr. Gunderson, who is the only one I can think of who might have that much money to lend. See what he says to you."

Doc said, "Is that all you have to say?"

"It is all. But I would advise you to think it over carefully before you get up on the witness stand."

He went out, crossed the parlor, and stepped out onto the porch. He was sweating, but he felt clammy cold. His knees were shaking, and so were his hands. He was scared. He was more scared than he had ever been before in his life.

CHAPTER

9

Daisy Middleton tried to sleep, but she couldn't. She still felt dizzy from the liquor she had drunk, but she wasn't intoxicated. Not anymore. Not since Olaf Gunderson had made his threat.

She'd have to do what he told her to, she thought. She couldn't see any other way out of it. But every time she made up her mind to say what Gunderson had told her to say, she'd think of Arnold Means, quiet and decent, a man who had never hurt anyone. He had come to her aid unhesitatingly, even though he didn't know how many were waiting for him, or what they would do to him. Unarmed, he had come charging into that alley as if he did it every night of his life. Because he had, he now lay dead. And she was supposed to lie in order to save one of his killers from paying the penalty.

Despite the fact that she was a prostitute, Daisy was a moral person. She wouldn't steal, and she had never lied. Brock Davidson didn't have to check on her at the saloon, because she

was meticulous about giving him half of everything she earned, although, occasionally, she
didn't mind turning a trick away from the
saloon. She didn't owe Brock a split on that. As
for robbing drunks, she wouldn't think of it,
even though she knew most prostitutes did,
every chance they got.

Now, she was going to *have* to lie. Gunderson
would have her beaten if she did not, maybe even
killed. He had promised that, and she believed.

She got out of bed and began pacing nervously
back and forth. She went out behind the house
and pumped a bucket of water from the well. She
came in, washed in cold water, and brushed her
hair. She put it up in a bun on the back of her
neck.

She dressed carefully. Much as she hated it,
she couldn't see any way out. She'd just have to
say what Gunderson had told her to, even
though she suspected that Orvie Gunderson had
most likely been the one who administered the
kick that actually killed Arnold Means.

Suddenly she remembered the paper she had
signed for Mr. Diggs. He had read it to her, and
it had said that only Marvin Shapiro was
attacking her while the other three boys were
beating Arnold Means. She would have to see
Mr. Diggs and get that paper back before she
could make the statement Gunderson wanted
her to make.

She put the six double eagles into her purse.
She went out, closing the door behind her but

not locking it. She hurried north on F Street and turned on Texas Street toward the bank.

It was early afternoon, and she suddenly realized she was hungry. She'd go by the saloon after she had seen Diggs and get something from the free lunch counter, she thought. Then she'd go on to the jail and make the statement Gunderson insisted on.

She climbed the steps to Diggs' office. He was sitting at his desk. He did not get up as he would have for any other woman in Kiowa. He just nodded at her as she came in.

She took the money out of her purse and laid it on his desk. "I can't take this, Mr. Diggs, and I've got to have that paper back."

Diggs frowned and shook his head. "I'm afraid it's too late for that. You signed your name. I've got the statement in my safe, and I intend to use it at the trial."

Daisy felt trapped. She said anxiously, "You don't understand, Mr. Diggs. I got to change what I said on that paper. Mr. Gunderson came to see me. He said if I didn't say his boy Orvie was down on the ground with Marv and me, then he was going to have me beat half to death."

"Gunderson said that?"

"Yes, sir. So you see why I got to have that paper back. I'm scared, Mr. Diggs. Mr. Gunderson will do what he says he'll do."

Diggs stubbornly shook his head. He picked up the money and held it out to her. "You'd better take this back. We've got a deal, and you can't go back on it."

Daisy felt tears burning in her eyes. She felt scared and helpless and alone. Mr. Diggs had been polite and respectful when he came to see her at her house. Now he was cold and almost rude. She shook her head. "I got to have that paper, Mr. Diggs. Don't you see? I got to have it. I got to change what it says."

"Well you can't have it. Now take your money and get out of here. I've got work to do."

She stood there a moment staring at him. Tears spilled out of her eyes and ran down her cheeks. He did not look up at her, but his hand was still extended, the six gold coins lying in it.

She turned and ran, weeping openly. She went out into the hall. Before going out the door onto the landing, she took a moment to try and compose herself. She dabbed at her eyes with a handkerchief. Then she went out and descended the outside stairs.

There was a normal flow of people in the street, and she could feel them staring curiously at her. Some of their stares were cold and disapproving, and she knew they blamed her, in part at least, for the death of Arnold Means. They didn't think she was worth what he had done for her. They didn't think she was worth dying for.

And they were right, she thought. She wasn't worth Arnold Means' life. Head down, she hurried along the street to the saloon. She went in.

Brock Davidson was behind the bar. "Hello, Daisy. How do you feel?"

She gave him a wan smile. "Rotten. I think I need something to eat." She crossed to the lunch counter and got herself some bread and cheese. She went behind the bar and drew herself a beer. Carrying sandwich and beer, she went to a table in a back corner of the room. Brock came over and sat down.

"Wyatt's got all of them but Orvie Gunderson."

She nodded. "I know."

"Did you know he put Olaf in jail in place of his son?"

She shook her head. The sheriff would probably put her in jail when he found out about the statement she had signed for Diggs, when she told him she now wanted to make a different one. She began to shiver, even though she wasn't cold.

Brock studied her worriedly. "Maybe you ought to see the Doc. You don't look so good."

"I'll be all right."

"Well, take the day off anyway."

She nodded dumbly. "Thanks, Mr. Davidson." She gulped the last of the bread and cheese and washed it down with the remains of the beer. She got up. She suddenly wanted to get this over with. She knew what she had to do. She had to tell the sheriff about the paper she had signed for Mr. Diggs. And she'd tell him she'd gotten to thinking about it and had decided she was wrong, that there had been two boys fighting with her while Arnold Means was being killed.

Diggs couldn't hurt her. Neither could Mr. Shapiro. But Gunderson could and would.

She reached the jail and went inside. Sheriff Wyatt was there, and so was Del Eggers, his part-time deputy. Wyatt got up from his desk. "Hello, Daisy. Ready to sign that statement?"

She nodded, and he held a chair for her beside his desk. She sat down. Wyatt got a pad of paper and a pencil. Daisy said, "There's something I've got to say."

"Go ahead."

"I signed another paper for Mr. Diggs."

"When?"

"This morning."

"Why? Did he offer you money for signing it?"

She nodded. "But I gave it back."

Wyatt looked angry. He asked, "What did the paper say?"

She hesitated. "Well, I can't read, but Mr. Diggs told me what it said. It said that Marvin Shapiro was wrestling with me on the ground all the time Mr. Means was being beat."

"And that's all?"

"Yes, sir."

"Well, that shouldn't be any problem, if that's what happened. I'll just write out another statement of all that happened, and you can sign it for me." He began to write.

Daisy said, "I've been thinkin' on it, sheriff, and I got to change what I said."

"What do you mean, change it?"

"Well, there was two boys struggling with me on the ground while Mr. Means was being beat."

Wyatt stared at her, and she felt her face grow hot. He said, "Don't tell me, let me guess. That second boy was Orvie Gunderson? Right?"

"Yes, sir."

Wyatt studied her for a long time. She could not meet his eyes. Finally he asked, "What did he offer you?"

"Offer me? Who?" She tried to sound innocent, but she knew it did not come off.

"Gunderson. How much did he offer you?"

She looked steadily at the floor and literally wrenched the words from deep inside of her. "He didn't offer me anything."

"Then he threatened you?"

"No, sir. He didn't threaten me."

"You're lying, Daisy."

"No, sir, Mr. Wyatt. I don't lie."

Wyatt shrugged. She was scared and exhausted, and he couldn't bring himself to try and browbeat the truth out of her. He got to his feet. "Daisy, I'm going to have to ask you to stay here for a while."

She nodded meekly. "Yes, sir."

Wyatt looked at Eggers, who was watching him puzzledly. "Don't let her leave, Del."

Eggers nodded, and Wyatt went out. He paused a moment in front of the jail, frowning. Then, hurrying, he headed for Judge Whelan's

94

house, two blocks east of the bank, on Texas Street.

The judge was taking an after-dinner nap in the parlor. His hair was tousled and his eyes sleepy when he answered the door. Wyatt said, "Sorry to bother you, Judge, but I want a warrant."

"Who for?"

"Daisy Middleton."

"On what kind of charge?"

"Prostitution will do."

"Why?"

"She's a witness, Judge, and I don't think she's safe running around loose. Shapiro tried to bribe her through Martin Diggs. And Gunderson has threatened her. She's half scared to death."

Judge Whelan nodded. He got his hat and came out onto the porch. "Come on up to the courthouse with me."

The courthouse occupied an entire block, bounded by Elm on the south, Maple on the north, B on the west, and A on the east. It was surrounded by lawn and trees. Wyatt and the judge crossed the lawn to the entrance and climbed the steps. Ten minutes later, Wyatt came out, a warrant for Daisy's arrest in his hand.

He hurried back toward the jail, stopping at the site of a house under construction almost directly behind Doc McNab's. Joe Shoemaker was sawing rafters in front of it, and Wyatt said,

"Can you spare a couple of hours this afternoon?"

"What for?"

"I've got to have a partition put up in the jail."

"What for?"

"I'm going to be holding Daisy Middleton, and the way it is, there's no privacy."

"You think she had something to do with what happened last night?"

Wyatt shook his head. "No. She's a witness, is all, and I don't want anything happening to her."

"Sure, I can do it, Wyatt. I'll hitch up a team and load a wagon with material. I'll be down in half an hour or so."

"Thanks." Wyatt headed for the jail.

Daisy was sitting in the same chair. She didn't look as if she had even moved. Wyatt felt sorry for her, and hated to tell her he was going to hold her in jail.

He sat down at his desk, facing her. "I'm afraid you're not going to like what I'm going to say to you."

She glanced up at him nervously.

"I'm going to have to hold you in jail until after the trial."

"In jail! Why?"

He showed the warrant to her. "This says prostitution. But that isn't the real reason. I just want to make sure nothing happens to you."

She looked as if he had struck her. He had expected anger, curses maybe, anything but this.

He said lamely, "It's for your own good, Daisy. I've got Joe Shoemaker coming down this afternoon to put a partition up so you'll have some privacy."

She did not reply. She just looked at him until he had to look away.

CHAPTER

10

Back in the cells, Olaf Gunderson yelled his name. Wyatt went back, and Gunderson said angrily, "You just going to let us sit here and starve? We ain't had dinner yet, and it's damn near two o'clock."

Wyatt said, "I'll see about it." He closed the door. He looked at Del Eggers. "Mind going over to the restaurant to get meals for the prisoners?"

Eggers was subdued, and Wyatt knew he had been thinking steadily about Carl and his chances ever since the boy had been brought to jail. But Eggers nodded his agreement, and Wyatt asked, "Daisy, would you mind helping him? There are four back there. We three make seven."

Del asked, "You want anything special, Matt?"

"Whatever they have." He wished he wasn't sheriff. Del was his best friend, and he had Del's son in jail, charged with murder. He liked Daisy, but he was going to have to put her in jail as well.

He wondered what had made him want to be sheriff in the first place. He must have been out of his mind.

The two left, and Wyatt sat down at the desk. They hadn't been gone five minutes when he heard the pounding of hoofs downstreet. He got up and went to the door. He opened it.

He'd known who it was the minute he heard the hoofs. It was Gunderson's crew, led by the foreman, Dutch Hahn. They pulled their plunging horses to a halt in front of the jail, and the cloud of dust they raised rolled on up the street. Wyatt looked for Orvie among them, but the boy wasn't there. Dutch asked, "You got the boss in there?"

Wyatt nodded.

"What have you charged him with?"

"I haven't charged him, but there are several things I can charge him with."

"I want to talk to him."

Wyatt shrugged. "All right. Come on in."

Dutch looked surprised. He got down off his horse and handed the reins up to one of the men nearby.

He came into the jail and Wyatt followed him. Halfway across the room he turned and looked at Wyatt questioningly. Wyatt said, "Leave your gun on the desk."

Hahn obeyed, then went back through the door leading to the cells. He closed it behind him, and immediately afterward Wyatt heard voices. Soon, he thought, he was going to have to get away and go out and arrest Orvie Gunderson. If he didn't, Orvie's father would see to it that his son got away. Far enough so that he'd never be found.

Hahn came out. He picked up his gun and shoved it into its holster. He said, "The old man wants to talk to you."

He went out, mounted his horse, and rode up the street, followed by the rest of the men. Wyatt went back to see what Gunderson wanted. The man said, "I want out of here."

Wyatt shook his head.

"You can't hold me forever without charging me."

"I can hold you seventy-two hours. After that, I've either got to charge you or turn you loose."

"Hahn's gone after Martin Diggs. He'll get me out. He'll get Judge Whelan to set bond for me."

"Fine. When he does, I'll turn you loose."

Gunderson scowled and muttered something Wyatt didn't hear. Wyatt said softly, "One of these days you're going to get what's coming to you, Mr. Gunderson. You've been throwing your weight around too long."

"You going to be the one to give it to me?"

Wyatt said, "It would be a pleasure. It would surely be a pleasure." He heard the front door and went back to the office. Eggers and Daisy had just come in, carrying piled up armloads of trays. They put them down on the desk.

Eggers carried four back to the cells, while Wyatt held the door open for him. Returning,

Wyatt said, "Eat, Daisy. It'll help the way you feel." He went to the door and peered outside. A wagon was coming down the street, driven by Joe Shoemaker. Shoemaker's helper, a middle-aged, dim-witted man named Horace Brown, was on the seat beside him. The wagon pulled up in front of the jail, and Horace got down and tied the team. He went around behind the wagon and began to unload the lumber. He piled it neatly on the walk against the front wall of the jail.

Gunderson's crew had disappeared into the saloon a block away, leaving their horses tied in front. Hahn's horse was tied in front of the bank.

He'd have to move fast, Wyatt thought. He'd have to get out to Gunderson's before Orvie got away. Hahn would send Diggs to the courthouse to post bail for Gunderson. Released, Gunderson would take his crew and get back out to the ranch. After that, the chances of capturing Orvie would be pretty slim.

Joe Shoemaker started to help Horace unload the wagon. Wyatt said, "Will you do something for me before you get started on that, Joe?"

"Sure. What do you want me to do?"

"Go up to the courthouse and ask Judge Whelan to stall on letting Diggs bail Gunderson out of jail."

"Sure, Matt." Sheomaker hurried away.

Staring up the street, Wyatt saw the two Means brothers come out of McNiel's furniture and undertaking establishment, two blocks up the street. They headed downstreet toward him, probably intending to stop at the saloon and have a drink. But with Gunderson's crew in there, Wyatt knew anything could happen, and probably would.

Hurriedly, he walked up the street to intercept them before they reached the saloon. Short of it, he beckoned them. They glanced into the saloon as they passed. They probably both needed a drink, after spending most of the day making funeral arrangements for Arnold, and he was sorry he had to deprive them of it. Bertram asked, "What do you want?"

Wyatt said, "I need some help. I've got Olaf Gunderson in jail, and his crew is in town to get him out. When they find out the judge won't set bail, they might try to take him out by force. I'd appreciate it if you two would stay there with Del Eggers until I get back."

"Back from where?"

"Gunderson's. I went out there after Orvie this morning, but Olaf kept me from arresting him. I've got to get back out before Gunderson's crew does, or I'll never be able to take him into custody."

The brothers looked at each other, then nodded simultaneously. "We'll help, sheriff."

"Good. Go on down there, then. Tell Eggers I asked you to help. Joe Shoemaker is going to be building a partition in the corridor between the cells so that Daisy will have some privacy."

"Daisy? You got her in jail?"

Wyatt nodded.

"Why? You think she had something to do with Arnold's death?"

"No. But she's the only witness, and I don't want anything to happen to her."

He walked the Means brothers to the jail. Gunderson's buggy was still standing in front, and so was Wyatt's horse. He untied the horse and led him back into the vacant lot beside the jail. There, he mounted, and keeping out of sight, rode south toward the railroad tracks. As soon as he was clear of town, he kicked the horse into a steady lope. He didn't know how much start he had, but he knew if Hahn and the rest of Gunderson's crew suspected what he was up to, they'd follow him.

He held the horse's gait as long as he dared, then let the horse walk a while. Yet, in spite of the way he hurried, it was after four when he reached Gunderson's.

He was a hundred yards from the house when he saw smoke puff from an upstairs window. An instant later the bullet struck fifteen feet in front of him, kicking a shower of dirt into his horse's face.

The animal reared, turned, and galloped back along the road. Wyatt didn't try to stop him. The shot had been a warning one. If he had continued toward the house, the second would have been aimed at him.

He continued back toward town, galloping, but as soon as a rise hid him from the house, he swung left, went through a wire gate, then rode

103

at a steady gallop toward the creek. Reaching it, he turned back toward the house, following the winding course of the creek at a steady trot. Orvie had fired that warning shot from his bedroom in the upstairs of the house. Having done so, and thinking he had scared the sheriff off, he would probably now try to flee. He'd head for the barn to get a horse, and he'd ride out as soon as he had saddled one.

Wyatt came into the grouped farm buildings from the direction of the creek. He approached the barn from the rear, dismounted, and left his horse's reins trailing on the ground. He drew his gun and hurried to the front of the barn.

The doors stood open. Wyatt glanced toward the house. He saw Mrs. Gunderson standing on the back stoop, wiping her hands on her apron, staring toward the barn. He knew instantly that Orvie had just gone into it.

He stepped into the barn. Orvie had a bridle on a horse, and was in the act of throwing a saddle blanket on. He froze, and turned, as Wyatt said, "Hold it, Orvie. I want you to come with me."

Orvie had no gun. He was too young to carry one. But there was a rifle in his saddle boot. The saddle lay on the barn floor, maybe ten feet away.

Orvie left the horse and stepped toward the saddle. Wyatt said sharply, "Dammit, I said hold it, and that's what I meant!"

Orvie froze. His eyes were panicked. He was

tense as a fiddle string. Wyatt didn't want to shoot him, and he hoped Orvie didn't force him to. He said, "All right. Stay right where you are." He crossed the barn toward Orvie's saddle, keeping his gun trained steadily on the boy. He reached the saddle, then stooped and withdrew the rifle from the boot.

For an instant, he took his eyes off the boy. He heard Orvie moving, and he knew immediately that he had made a bad mistake. Glancing up, he saw Orvie rushing toward him, a pitchfork in his hands.

Orvie was too close for him to get away. He arched his body to one side, letting himself fall, but he was too late. One tine of the filthy, manure-covered fork went into his left thigh, through clothes and flesh, and came out on the other side.

His falling body wrenched the fork out of Orvie's hands. The pain brought a cry out of him that was almost a scream. Recovering, slammed against a stall partition, he roared, "You son-of-a-bitch, stand still or I'll kill you where you stand!"

Something in the timbre of his voice made Orvie freeze exactly where he stood. Wyatt glanced down at the pitchfork, seeing how filthy it was, feeling it like a branding iron against his leg. Shuddering violently, he said savagely, "Get hold of it and pull it out. And if you try to ram it into me again, I'm going to let you have it right in the gut!"

Shaken and white, Orvie took hold of the handle and gave it a half-hearted pull. The pain made Wyatt's head reel. If Orvie didn't get the damn thing out soon, he was going to faint, and then the damned kid would get away. He gritted, "Pull, damn you! Yank it out!"

This time Orvie gave it a sudden yank and it came clear. Orvie staggered back, still holding to the fork. Wyatt said, "Turn your back to me and throw it clear across the barn."

He could feel blood running down his leg, now, front and rear. He hoped the wound would bleed a lot because that would cleanse it, but he knew he didn't have much time. He had to get back to town immediately so that Doc could clean it out thoroughly. And as dizzy as he felt, he knew he might pass out at any time.

Orvie flung the fork across the barn. Harshly Wyatt said, "Now saddle up. And by God, if you try one more thing, you're going to be dead."

Subdued, Orvie returned to his horse. He flung the saddle up and cinched it down. Wyatt followed him out of the barn. He said, "My horse is around on that side. Go get him."

Orvie obeyed. He came back, leading Wyatt's horse. Holding the reins of Orvie's horse, Wyatt climbed stiffly into his saddle. When he was settled, he said, "Mount up."

Orvie did, and Wyatt handed him the reins. He said, "Let's go. Remember, I can kill you before you go a dozen yards."

Orvie headed along the road toward town,

with Wyatt right behind. Wyatt wanted to stay on the road until they were out of sight of the house. After that, he intended to leave it, and reach town by cutting straight across country where there would be no chance of running into Gunderson's crew returning to the ranch.

Looking down at the blood seeping through his pants, at the manure surrounding the hole, he felt a vast disgust. There wasn't a filthier wound in the world than the one he had just sustained, and he knew how terribly dangerous a wound it was. He could get blood-poisoning, lockjaw, gangrene. He could lose the leg. He could even lose his life.

Furiously he glared at the broad, muscled back of the outsized fifteen-year-old ahead of him, half wishing Orvie would make a break so that he could shoot.

CHAPTER

11

Orvie Gunderson was silent and sullen all the way to town, but there was a lack of fear in him that Wyatt found very irritating. Orvie knew his father was going to stand by him, and he had unlimited confidence in the power his father could wield when he wanted to. He figured he was going to get off without even going to prison.

The pain in Wyatt's leg was a terrible, constant ache. He felt like a man who has been bitten by a rattlesnake. The poison was seeping steadily through his body, but he didn't know what he could do about it.

He kept his horse at a gallop most of the way, willing to ruin the horse, if necessary, to save his leg, and perhaps his life. At times he had to cut Orvie's horse across the rump with the barrel of the rifle that he now carried in his hand.

He knew that Gunderson's crew, led by the foreman, Dutch Hahn, if still in town, would forcibly prevent him from getting Orvie into the jail. Hahn knew without being told what the old man expected of him. And Hahn was loyal.

He returned to the road cautiously as he drew near town. It was late, nearly six o'clock. The sun hung low in the western sky, enlarged and turned orange by dust suspended in the air.

The town looked normal. At six, which was suppertime, the streets were all but deserted, but there were an unusual number of horses racked in front of the Ace High Saloon.

Gunderson's crew, he thought, and wondered if he'd be able to make it to the jail without being seen. Almost imperceptibly, he shook his head. Their horses might be tied in front of the saloon, but they had missed him by now, and one or more of them would certainly be keeping watch. A single gunshot from the lookout or lookouts, and the rest of them would erupt from the saloon.

He would need some kind of diversion. Capturing Orvie, he'd taken this dirty pitchfork wound in the leg, and he had no intention of giving him up. As they rode across the railroad tracks, he said, "Swing left along the tracks."

Orvie turned his head. "Why? What are you gonna do?"

"Never mind!" Wyatt's voice was almost a snarl. "And don't get any ideas of trying to get away from me. My leg hurts like bloody hell and, as far as I'm concerned, you're just another killer."

Scowling, Orvie turned obediently along the tracks. Wyatt wondered what kind of diversion he could create that would enable him to get

Orvie safely to the jail. A fire was the only thing he could come up with, but he knew it had to be one that destroyed nothing of value and that, furthermore, could not spread and threaten the rest of the town.

Nestled down against the bed of Kiowa Creek, straight ahead of him, was a small tarpaper shack, abandoned now, which had been used sometimes in the past by tramps that came through on the trains. It would do, he thought. The tarpaper would make a lot of black, oily smoke, and once it got started, it ought to shoot flames fifty feet into the air. The instant the Gunderson crew saw that the shack was the source of the fire, they'd know they had been duped, of course, but by then Wyatt figured he could have Orvie safely locked in jail.

He rode up alongside Orvie and said harshly, "Give me your reins."

Orvie obeyed. Wyatt dismounted stiffly, in front of the shack, nearly falling when he put his weight on his injured leg. His face was gray, and there was a shine of sweat on it. He deliberately knotted the reins of his own horse to those of Orvie's horse. He pulled the knot as tight as he could. He said, "You stay in the saddle. Make any move to get down, and I'll blow your goddam head off. Is that understood?"

Orvie did not reply. Wyatt fumbled in his pocket for matches and went into the shack. He propped the door open so that he could see Orvie while he worked. Fortunately, there was a litter of dry grass and paper in one corner, probably a rat's nest. He dropped a lighted match into it and watched the flames lick up.

Quickly, he went outside and tore some pieces of tarpaper off the shack. He took them inside and fed the flames with them. In minutes, the whole side of the shack was ablaze.

He went back outside and, as quickly as he could, untied the reins, but this time he did not hand Orvie's reins up to him. Holding them, he mounted his own horse and dug heels into his sides. He rode him down into the bed of Kiowa Creek and forced him to lope, despite the brush and rocks and the unevenness of the ground.

He had gone no more than a quarter mile when he heard the church bell begin to clang. Urgently. The way it always did when there was a fire.

Something made him look around. Orvie was in the act of jumping from his horse. He had not yet left the animal when Wyatt yelled, "Hold it! Hit the ground and by God you're dead!"

Orvie grabbed his saddle horn and pulled himself awkwardly back upright. Wyatt returned his attention to the land ahead. He was above the jail already, perhaps even with the saloon. Glancing back, he could see the pillar of black smoke boiling into the air.

At the tip of the gulch in which the creek ran, he halted his horse. Give them enough time, he thought. Let them get well below the jail. When he judged the time was right, he kicked his horse into motion, dragging Orvie's along behind.

He came into town on Texas Street, and rode at a steady lope along it to the alley behind the Ace High Saloon. He cut into the alley, still loping, his eyes shifting anxiously to right and left. He reached the lower end of the alley where the attack on Daisy and Arnold Means had taken place last night, and glanced back at Orvie's face. It was almost green, and Orvie's eyes were rigidly straight ahead. If he'd had any doubt about Orvie's guilt before, it was now gone.

There was a lot of yelling from the direction of the railroad tracks, and the church bell still rang steadily. The fire engine rattled past on Kansas Street, its bell also clanging frantically. He'd timed it just about right, Wyatt thought as he rode across Longhorn Street and into the alley behind the jail.

Reaching the jail itself, he cut through the vacant lot beside it and reached the street in front. People were running past, but he saw no sign of Dutch Hahn or any of Gunderson's crew.

To Orvie Gunderson, he said, "Get down! Into the jail." Orvie slid out of his saddle. His eyes said he was debating flight, but he changed his mind when he saw how steadily Wyatt's rifle barrel covered him. Wyatt slid from his own saddle, nearly falling when his leg threatened to collapse as he hit the ground. He tried the jail door and found it locked.

It opened almost immediately, and Del Eggers

stood framed in it. Wyatt said, "Put Orvie in a cell."

Orvie went in and Wyatt followed him. He stood with his weight on his good leg as Eggers herded Orvie back into a cell. Wyatt could see that the partition was finished, and supposed that Daisy was locked safely in.

He walked back to look at the partition. He could see into the cells occupied by the men, but not into Daisy's cell. Gunderson glared at him. "You dirty son-of-a-bitch!"

That brought a grin of triumph to his face. Eggers pushed Orvie into a cell, then closed and locked the door. He came back along the corridor. Both men went into the office and closed the door behind. Eggers asked, "You set that fire?"

Wyatt nodded.

Eggers said, "Good thing. They had a man on top of the building across the street. The minute he saw you, he'd have fired a warning shot. You'd never have reached the jail."

"I figured it might be that way. Where's Bertram and Lane?"

"They went to dinner. Said they'd be right back and that they'd bring supper for the prisoners."

Wyatt said, "You go home when they get back. I've got to get up to Doc's."

Eggers glanced down at his leg. "What happened?"

"Pitchfork. A dirty one. That damn kid drove

it clear through my leg."

Eggers whistled sympathetically. "Go ahead. Don't worry about things down here."

Wyatt stepped out into the street. He heard the door bolt shoot home behind him. Eggers was taking no chances. Eggers was a damn good man. He glanced downstreet and saw Dutch Hahn coming, the crew behind him like an angry mob. He waited because he didn't want them to think he'd run from them. They reached him and Dutch said angrily, "You set that son-of-a-bitch, didn't you?"

Wyatt nodded.

"And you've got Orvie locked up in jail?"

Wyatt nodded again.

"We'll bust the damn thing open like a tomato can."

"Better not." He stared at Hahn a moment, and it was Hahn who looked away. Wyatt said, "That horse belongs to Gunderson. You can take the buggy back too."

He mounted his own horse, trying not to let Hahn and his men see how badly he was hurt. He rode up the street toward Doc McNab's. At the corner of Texas Street and Kansas, he met the Means brothers coming from the restaurant. Both of them were carrying trays. Bertram looked up at him and asked, "Get him?"

Wyatt nodded. "He's down in jail."

Bertram studied his pain-wracked face. "You hurt?"

"Orvie ran a pitchfork into my leg."

"Better get Doc to look at it."

"That's where I'm headed now. I told Del to go home and eat as soon as you two got back. Keep the door locked, and don't let anybody in but Del or me."

"Don't worry." The ghost of a grin hovered on Bertram's mouth. "You set that fire, didn't you?"

Wyatt nodded. "I knew they'd never let me get to the jail with Orvie unless I did something to draw them off."

"Go on up to Doc's. Lane and me will look after things until you get back."

Wyatt continued up the street. He stopped in front of Doc's house and slid off his horse. He tied the animal and went up the walk.

The sun was setting now, staining the clouds a brilliant orange. Mrs. McNab let him in and led him back to Doc's office. Doc looked at the manure and blood on his pants leg and said, "Pitchfork?"

Wyatt nodded.

"Go clear through?"

"Uh-huh."

"Orvie?"

"Yeah. Now get at it, will you?"

"Sure. Take off your pants."

Wyatt pulled off his boots, then unbuckled his gun belt and took off his pants. His underwear was soaked with blood. Doc said, "Bled good. That helps." He ripped the leg of Wyatt's underwear all the way around, then pulled it off. The wound was a small, bluish hole, from which a little dark red blood seeped.

Doc motioned toward the couch. "Lie down. This is going to hurt."

Wyatt lay down on the couch. Doc stirred up something in a glass and gave it to him. "It's bitter, but drink it down."

Wyatt did, grimacing. Doc busied himself across the room with his instruments. Wyatt smelled something acrid and strong. It seemed like Doc fiddled around for a long, long time. Wyatt's head began to whirl. The leg had almost stopped hurting and he felt strange. Doc came back, carrying something in his hand. He said, "There's some rails on the cot. Hold onto them. It'll help."

Wyatt dropped his hands and got hold of the cot rails. He knew what was coming, and he braced himself for it.

When it came, it was ten times worse than he had thought it was going to be. It was like a red-hot iron, jammed straight into his leg. He yelled involuntarily and gripped the rails with all his strength. Doc had hold of his leg now, raising it.

Again, the red hot pain stabbed through his leg, this time from the rear. Only this time Wyatt fainted. His head fell back, and his hands relaxed their ironlike grip on the rails of the cot.

When he came to, the leg hurt like bloody hell. He was soaked with sweat. Doc was working across the room. Wyatt raised his head and looked down at his leg. It was bandaged now. He glanced across the room at Doc. "What did you do?"

"Cleaned it. Put a drain in it. You let a thing like that close up and you'll lose the leg."

"Is that what hurt so bad?"

"Uh-huh. There's two, actually. One in front and one in back. You come back in the morning."

Wyatt sat up. His head whirled. He reached for his pants, stood up and put them on. He buckled on his gun, then sat down and put on his boots. He asked, "Will it be all right?"

Doc said, "I don't know. We'll just have to watch it and see."

"You're the cheerful one, aren't you?"

Doc handed him a crutch. "You'll need this."

Wyatt said, "I will like hell. It's going to be hard enough keeping the lid on things for the next few hours without going around all crippled up." He went to the window and looked outside, surprised to see that the sky was wholly dark.

CHAPTER

12

Behind him, Wyatt heard Doc say, "Matt. . . ."

He turned his head. He knew instantly that something was wrong. Doc was looking at the floor, apparently unable to meet his eyes. He felt a strange uneasiness as he said, "What?"

"About Arnold's death. . . ."

"What about it?"

"I was probably a little hasty. You know how that can be. I was shocked to find him lying down there in the alley, shocked at what had happened to him."

"What are you trying to say?" Wyatt's voice was cold.

"Just that I could be wrong."

"Wrong about what he said?" A feeling of disillusionment flooded over Wyatt now. Sol Shapiro had reached Doc, just the way he'd reached Daisy earlier. Money could do a lot of things. It could buy freedom for a murderer. In this case, it apparently had. But he hadn't believed that Doc was for sale. He'd never have believed that.

Doc was shaking his head. "No. I didn't make any mistake about what he said. He said Marv, and Frank, all right."

"What then?"

"It's the cause of death."

Wyatt said sarcastically, "You're not going to tell me he died from natural causes?"

Doc's face flushed painfully. He still did not raise his glance and look at Wyatt. He said, "No. But I was hasty when I said those boys kicked him to death. I was angry, and I had no right to speak that injudiciously."

"And now that you've had time to think it all over judiciously, what do you say?"

"That it could have been an accident."

"Accident? For Christ's sake, man, he was beaten to death."

Doc stubbornly shook his head. "He died of head injuries."

"Well, kicked to death then. Or battered to death. What's the difference?"

"Head injuries can be caused in a number of different ways."

"All right." Wyatt's voice was bitter. "Let's hear your new story about how he died."

Doc glanced up now, a spark of anger in his eyes. "You've got no right to talk to me that way."

"Why not? It's pretty damn plain what has happened. Come on, let's hear what you're now going to say caused Arnold's death."

"It *could* have been an accident."

"Sure. A man's kicked to death by three vicious kids, and you say it could have been an accident. Dammit, it was murder! Cold-blooded murder. Murder in the first degree. Those kids are going to hang. All four of them." He realized that anger had made his own statement more intemperate than he had meant it to be. He didn't want the four boys to hang. He only wanted some kind of justice for Arnold Means.

Doc repeated stubbornly, "It could have been an accident. I examined Arnold more carefully before I sent him down to McNiel's."

"And what were your conclusions the second time?"

"That he died from a single blow."

"Then he wasn't literally beaten to death, the way you said earlier?"

Doc shook his head. "Death is usually caused by a single blow."

"But there were more blows than one?"

"There were bruises and contusions, yes. But he died from that single blow."

"One of the many?"

"One blow." Doc's voice had a dogged stubbornness about it now.

"And how was that one blow administered?"

Doc shrugged. "It could have been administered in a number of different ways."

Wyatt said, "Don't tell me. Let me guess. A fall?"

Doc's face was red and sweating now, and he kept his glance determinedly on the floor. He nodded. "It could have been caused by a fall."

"By hitting his head on the ground?"

"No. A rock or some other hard object. I imagine there are plenty of things lying around in that alley."

"Where was the injury located that caused Arnold's death?"

"The worst wound appeared to be in the back."

"Appeared to be? Aren't you sure?"

"No doctor could be sure. I would have to assume that the worst looking injury was the one that caused his death."

"And I thought Arnold was a friend of yours."

"He was."

"If that's the way you treat your friends, I think I'll just be your enemy."

Doc shrugged, glanced quickly at Wyatt, then looked away again. "Suit yourself."

"How much did Shapiro offer you? How much is justice for Arnold worth?"

Doc threw back his head. His eyes blazed at Wyatt now. "Damn you, don't talk that way to me! You know damned well I wouldn't lie for money!"

"You're not lying now?"

Doc shook his head. "I'm stating possibilities. You know as well as anybody that medicine isn't an exact science. No doctor can put an exact cause on everything. There are lots of things no doctor knows."

"Maybe we'll get another doctor in here to

look at Arnold Means. Maybe, by God, we'll find out how much some other doctor knows."

There was silence for a long moment. At last Doc said pleadingly, "Why can't you just take my word? Those boys didn't mean to kill. It had to be an accident."

"Why would Sol Shapiro pay you to say this now? Daisy said Marv was struggling with her all the time."

"Sol Shapiro did not pay me!"

"Then why the lie?" Wyatt crossed the room to where Doc stood. The pain in his leg was like a red-hot iron. And suddenly, all that had happened throughout the long, long day broke the thread of his restraint. He grabbed the front of Doc's shirt and glared into the older man's eyes. He said savagely, "Damn you, I was rousted out of bed at one o'clock this morning, and I've been up ever since. I've been knocked cold by Olaf Gunderson, and had a pitchfork run through my leg. I'm through playing games. Who bribed you to lie and with what?"

"Nobody . . . I. . . ."

"You want to go to jail too? All right, come on." He dragged Doc toward the door.

"No! I'll tell you! I'll tell you!"

"Tell me then!" Wyatt did not let go.

"It was Sol Shapiro! But I didn't do it for money, Matt!"

"What then? Talk, damn you!"

"The house. Shapiro's bank holds the mortgage, and it's due in a couple of months. He said he wouldn't renew, and he said if he refused, no other bank would lend me the money to pay him off."

Wyatt let him go. "Why the hell should Sol be so concerned? Marv never touched Arnold, if what Daisy says is true."

"He said that attacking Daisy was a felony, and that Marv was just as guilty as if he'd helped beat Arnold."

Wyatt nodded. "It's true in theory, but juries don't always go along with it."

He sat down suddenly on the couch. It seemed like a month since he'd been wakened early this morning by Daisy's screaming outside his door.

In a day, he'd done all right, too. He'd captured all the boys. He'd lodged them safely in jail. He'd built up his case. He'd done everything he should.

He shook his head almost imperceptibly. No, if he'd done all he should, he wouldn't have lost his witnesses. He should have known how hard both Shapiro and Gunderson would fight to save their only sons. He should have anticipated the lengths to which they were both prepared to go. But he hadn't, and now it was too late. If the case went to trial tomorrow, the boys would all get off. Arnold Means' death would be called an accident. They'd be sentenced to thirty days in jail for simple assault, and that would be the end of it.

Except that he knew it wouldn't be the end of it. Arnold Means had two brothers, and neither of them was as peacefully inclined as Arnold had been. Furthermore, Arnold had had a lot of friends. In a case this clear cut, they wouldn't stand for Arnold's killers getting off practically scot free.

He got to his feet wearily. More than anything, he wanted to lie down and go to sleep, but he knew it wasn't going to be possible for a while. He said, "You know what's going to happen if those boys get off, don't you?"

Doc looked puzzled and confused.

"All hell is going to break loose in this town. The damn kids might be lynched. Arnold Means had a lot of friends, and he has two brothers that are mad as hell."

Doc didn't say anything. Disgustedly, Wyatt limped to the door and went outside.

For a moment he stood on the porch in the cool night air. A light breeze blew from the south, carrying some kind of fragrance, a fragrance he couldn't immediately identify. He walked to the street and untied his horse. Stiffly, and with difficulty, he swung to the saddle. Bandaged, the leg was even stiffer than it had been before. He ought to go home and change clothes, he thought. He smelled of manure from rolling around in the Gunderson barn with Orvie.

He rode down Kansas Street toward the jail. There was a lot of activity in the saloon, and the tie rail in front was packed. At the bank corner, he heard running feet and glanced toward the sound.

A woman, or girl, was coming toward him, running in the darkness. Almost immediately he recognized Josie Eggers. He pulled his horse to a halt and slid to the ground. Her voice, breathless and scared, came out of the darkness, "Matt? Is that you?"

"Uh-huh. It's me." He took a step toward her, and she said, with immediate concern, "You're hurt!"

"Orvie Gunderson rammed a pitchfork through my leg."

She reached him and stood there looking up. "You've got no business walking around. You ought to be in bed."

"Later."

"I just got back. I just heard. Did they really do it, Matt? Did Carl have a part in it?"

"I'm afraid he did."

"How do you know?"

"The other boys named him. And he ran."

"That doesn't necessarily mean. . . ." But he could tell from her voice that she knew Carl had had a part in it. She knew the four boys ran together. She asked, "What's going to happen?"

"They'll go to trial. I guess it will be up to the judge."

"Could they . . . I mean, at their age, would the judge . . . ?"

He knew what she meant. He said, "Probably not. Because of their ages."

She was shivering as if she were very cold. She asked, "Can I see him?"

Wyatt shook his head. "Your pa wouldn't let you go in there. I've got Carl and the other three, and I've got Daisy and Olaf Gunderson. It's no place for you right now."

She was silent for a long time. At last she said, "He'll go to prison, won't he, Matt?"

"I'm afraid he will."

"Oh, Lord! Why? Why would he do a thing like that?"

Wyatt couldn't answer her. He said, "Let me take you home."

"Your leg. . . ."

"Walking will do it good. Take the stiffness out."

"Isn't a wound like that awfully dangerous? A dirty pitchfork and all?"

"It can be, I guess."

Trailing his horse, he walked along the street with her toward the Eggers' house. Reaching it, she stopped. She looked up at him, her face pale and lovely in the near darkness. He leaned down and kissed her lightly on the mouth. "Don't worry, Josie. Any more than you have to."

She began to cry. He put his arms around her and held her for a moment. At last she pulled away, and dried her eyes with her hands. "I'll be all right."

He watched her go up the walk toward the house, feeling lousy, feeling somehow as if he was to blame for what was happening.

CHAPTER

13

Wyatt had not eaten, and while he suspected that food might only make him sick, he knew he'd feel a hell of a lot worse if he didn't get something into his stomach.

He tied his horse in front of the hotel and went in. He crossed the tiled floor of the lobby and went into the dining room. He couldn't help limping a little, but he tried to keep the limp from being noticeable.

It was late for supper, but there were still half a dozen men in the hotel dining room. He didn't know any of them. He supposed they were salesmen passing through. One looked as if he might be a cattle buyer, though it was early in the year for cattle buyers to be showing up.

He sat down at a table near the window, so that he could look out into the street. The waitress, a Mexican girl named Dolores Sanchez, came to take his order. Her eyes were red from crying, and he knew why. She had known Frank Avila, and had gone to the local dances with him. To have him accused of murder, and in jail, must terrify her. To know he had confessed to the attempted rape of Daisy Middleton must have hurt her considerably.

Wyatt asked, "What have you got tonight, Dolores?"

"Roast beef, chicken and dumplings."

"I'll take the roast beef. And coffee."

"Yes, sir." She hesitated a moment, frightened but also determined. Finally she asked, "What will happen to Frank?"

"Depends on the jury, Dolores, but he's in pretty deep. The least he'll get will be a long prison term."

White-faced, she nodded. She turned and hurried away.

The man who looked like a cattle buyer had been watching him. Now he got up and approached. He said, "You must be the sheriff. I see you're wearing a star."

Wyatt nodded and extended his hand. "Excuse me for not getting up. I've got a sore leg."

"That's all right. Mind if I sit down?"

Wyatt shook his head. He did mind, but he didn't want to be rude. The man sat down. "I'm Ralph Griffin."

Wyatt's glance was questioning. The man said, "I just got in on the train this afternoon. I heard about what happened here last night."

Wyatt couldn't help feeling puzzled. He wondered what the man was leading up to. Griffin said, "Damn shame — a good man like Means getting himself killed over a lousy whore."

Wyatt felt a slight irritation. He said, "He did what any decent man would do. I can't see that the morals of the woman he was defending have anything to do with it."

"No offense." Griffin grinned knowingly. "I take it you know the girl."

Wyatt asked, "Who the hell are you, anyway? And what business is this of yours?"

"I'm a newspaperman. Kansas City Globe. When the train stopped here, I heard about what had happened, so I got off. I thought there might be a story in it."

Wyatt saw Dolores coming with his food. He said, "It's been a long day, Mr. Griffin. I'm hungry and I'm tired. If you don't mind, I'd like to eat my supper in peace."

Griffin stood up. "Of course, Sheriff. Of course. I'll be around. I'll talk to you another time."

"What about? By now you must have all the facts."

"I just know what happened last night. Not what's going to happen in the next few days."

"What *is* going to happen?"

Griffin spread his hands. "Anything could happen, Sheriff. It's an explosive situation."

He left, crossed the room to where he had been sitting, and sat down again. Wyatt watched Dolores put his supper in front of him, a light frown on his face. He knew the situation in Kiowa was explosive, but he hadn't realized it was noticeable enough to be apparent to a total stranger in town.

He discovered that he was hungry. The first few bites caused him to feel a little nauseous, but after that it passed. He finished eating and sipped the scalding black coffee. He felt better. His leg ached and throbbed, and he still felt tired, but he wasn't as irritable as he had been when he came in.

He left money on the table and got up. Griffin, across the room, rose at the same time. Wyatt went out. He untied his horse but he did not mount.

There were a lot of people in the street for this time of night. The saloon was noisier than usual, perhaps because the doors were open to the warm night air. Passing, Wyatt stopped suddenly. Shapiro had reached Daisy and Doc. He wondered if he had reached Brock Davidson as well.

He tied his horse and went into the saloon. It was more crowded than usual, and everyone was talking about the crime. Brock Davidson was tending bar. Ned Leeds was helping him. Wyatt went to the end of the bar and signaled Brock, who came immediately.

Wyatt said, "Can you take a minute, Brock?"

"Sure. Ned can look after things."

"I want to talk to you. I'd like to get your story, and tomorrow I'd like to have you come by the jail and sign a statement."

Brock glanced at Ned as if he would like to get

away. Wyatt wondered why. Brock asked, "What do you want to know?"

"When you locked up . . . was that when you heard Daisy scream?"

"Yeah. She was down at the corner. She saw me, I guess, and started yelling for me."

"All right. And you ran down that way. How did Daisy look?"

"What do you mean how did she look?"

"Well, I mean how much did she have on? How did she look?"

"She didn't have much on."

"Was she naked?"

"Damn near."

"What did she have on?"

"Hell man, I didn't notice. She was screeching about Arnold Means bein' hurt. All I wanted to do was get back into the alley an' see how bad."

Wyatt waited a moment, studying the man. At last he asked the question he had come in here to ask, "What do you think, Brock? Do you think she was attacked? Do you think those kids tried to force her against her will?" There was no doubt in Wyatt's mind, but he had to know if Shapiro had reached the man.

Brock was watching Ned pour a drink for a man at the other end of the bar. He said, without looking at Wyatt, "Hell, Matt, I don't know. They might. The only thing is, I don't know why they'd have to. Both Orvie and Marv have plenty of money to spend. Frank worked for Arnold in the hardware store, and if he'd wanted to pay

Daisy, he could have dug up a dollar easy enough. I don't know about Carl, but his family ain't exactly poor. I don't see why any of those kids would have to force Daisy, and I'm not too damned sure they did."

"You think she went into the alley of her own free will?"

Brock shrugged. "It's possible."

"Then why would she scream?"

"Maybe the boys got too rough for her. Maybe they tore her clothes. Kids that age get pretty worked up, Matt."

"Is that what you're going to say in court?"

"Sure. It's the truth."

"And I suppose you'll also say that Daisy had a habit of trying to make a few dollars on the side — money she didn't have to share with you?"

"Sure. She did."

Wyatt asked, "You seen Sol Shapiro today?"

Brock hadn't looked straight at him since he came to the end of the bar. He didn't do so now. "Sure. He's been in. Why?"

"You talk to him?"

"Sure. I talk to most of the customers."

"Did he offer you money, or threaten you?"

Now Brock raised his glance and looked Wyatt straight in the eye. He said, "What the hell are you talking about?" He tried desperately to hold Wyatt's glance, but he failed and had to look away.

Wyatt said, "He tried to bribe Daisy and he

threatened Doc. I wouldn't be surprised if he'd try bribing you. What did he offer you?"

"You're crazy. He didn't offer me anything."

"Then why can't you look me straight in the eye?"

Brock's neck turned red. He growled, "I can." He raised his glance and met that of the sheriff. He held it, with grim determination, for almost a minute. Then he looked away again. Wyatt asked, "What did he offer you?"

"He didn't offer me anything."

"Do you owe him money?"

"Sure. There's a mortgage on the saloon. What's wrong with that?"

Wyatt said, "You know what can happen to you if you lie on the witness stand?"

"No. What?"

"You can go to prison. I think the maximum is five years. Of course, the judge might only give you three."

"Lie?" Brock raised his glance. This time his eyes held Wyatt's without fear. "It ain't really a lie. Daisy might have agreed to take on them boys. They might've gotten too rough for her and torn her clothes. That would've made her yell. Clothes cost money, and Daisy wasn't exactly getting rich."

"Or she might have been dragged into the alley against her will?"

"Sure. I guess that's possible."

"That's what Daisy says happened. You think she's lying? Was she supposed to split with you when she made some money away from the saloon?"

Brock shook his head. "What she did away from here was her own business. Only she was supposed to be here certain hours. That was all."

"Daisy doesn't usually leave before you close, does she?"

"Nope. She usually leaves when I lock up."

"Why did she leave early last night?"

"She said she was tired."

"She do that often? Leave early because she's tired?"

Brock shook his head. "Not often."

"Then if she was so tired, it's not likely she'd have considered taking on four boys in an alley, is it? Not even when the whole four dollars would belong to her."

Brock scowled, then reluctantly shook his head. "I guess not."

Wyatt nodded. He said, "Shapiro's trying to save his boy, and I guess I can't really blame him for that. But I blame him for how he's doing it. Just remember, when you come down to the office to sign that statement tomorrow, that this saloon won't do you any good in prison." Brock looked up and Wyatt held his glance inflexibly as he said, "And if anybody lies and gets those kids off, I'm personally going after whoever it was that lied. I'm going to see that they pay the penalty."

Brock said, "That all?"

"It's all. Be down at the office first thing

tomorrow. I'll have the statement all made out, just the way you told me the story the first time I talked to you."

"You're really trying to hang 'em, aren't you."

"No. I'm just trying to make sure that their trial isn't influenced — one way or the other. That's my job."

Brock moved away, and Wyatt walked through the crowd and out of the saloon. A couple of men tried to question him, but he didn't answer them. He went out into the street, found a cigar in his vest pocket, and lighted it. It was a little crumpled, probably from the fight with Orvie, but it was smokable. He puffed two or three times and then untied his horse and headed for the jail.

Eggers opened the door for him. The Means brothers were gone. Eggers said, "Sol Shapiro was here a while ago."

"What did he want?"

"Wanted to see Gunderson."

"You didn't let him?"

Eggers nodded. "Well, yes I did. I didn't see any harm in it. I searched him first to make sure he didn't have no gun on him."

Wyatt was irritated, but he tried not to let it show. He nodded. "All right, Del. You can go home now if you want."

Eggers nodded. "You going to sleep here tonight?"

Wyatt nodded. "Stable my horse for me when you leave, will you? Feed him some grain and

135

throw him down some hay. And give him a drink."

"Sure, Matt."

"The Means brothers stay in town?"

"Uh-huh. They're up at the hotel."

"All right. Good night, Del."

Eggers went to the door. He paused with his hand on the knob. "How long do you think they'll get?"

"I wish I could tell you, Del, but I can't. I know Carl pretty good though, and I'll speak up for him at the trial."

Del Eggers nodded, a shocked and confused man. "Thanks, Matt. Thanks." He went out and closed the door. Wyatt crossed the room and bolted it.

CHAPTER

14

Glancing at the clock, Wyatt was surprised to see that it was not yet nine o'clock. It seemed like weeks since Daisy had gotten him out of bed this morning, banging on the door and screaming hysterically. Enough things had happened, it seemed, to fill a lifetime. And he had the uneasy feeling that it had only begun. A lot more was going to happen in the next few days.

Back in the cells, Olaf Gunderson bawled, "Matt! Hey Matt!"

Wearily he limped to the door and opened it. "What do you want?"

"I want to talk to you."

"What about?" Wyatt looked at him suspiciously. Orvie was in the same cell with his father. He sat on the couch, his head in his hands.

"About getting out of here."

"Not a chance."

"Matt, I'm sorry for all the trouble I gave you. I honest to God am. But hell, put yourself in my place. Suppose you had a boy and somebody

137

came out and said he'd killed somebody. You'd do whatever you could to protect him, wouldn't you?"

Grudgingly Wyatt said, "Maybe."

"And you can't blame me for trying to get the straight of it out of that . . . out of Daisy Middleton."

"The hell I can't. You tried to bribe her, and you threatened her. I don't exactly call that getting the straight of it."

"Matt, I don't want you to think I'm threatening you, but Dutch Hahn and the boys are in town. And there's no telling what they'll do. If I was out, I could send 'em home."

"You could, but would you?" Wyatt suddenly realized that he hadn't seen a single one of the Gunderson crew in the saloon. Either they had gone home, or they were planning something.

"Matt, I may be a lot of things, but I'm not a liar. You know that."

Wyatt stared at him doubtfully. His leg ached ferociously, and his disposition was terrible. He was dead for sleep. Maybe if he let Gunderson go, and the man got his crew out of town, things would quiet down.

But he didn't wholly trust Gunderson, and he didn't agree with Gunderson's statement that he wasn't a liar. Gunderson was whatever he had to be to get his way. If it took lying to get Orvie off, he'd lie.

He nodded reluctantly. "All right. On condition that you take your crew and get out of town."

"I will. I swear it. Thanks, Matt. You won't regret it."

"I sure as hell hope I won't. But don't get the idea that I'm dropping charges against you."

"I'll take my medicine when the time comes for it."

Wyatt stared at him a moment, suspiciously. Gunderson was being too damned agreeable, and it was completely out of character. But he knew there was nothing to be gained by keeping Gunderson in jail. If he was free, he just might keep his crew from making the trouble worse.

He unlocked the cell. Gunderson stepped out. Wyatt watched him warily as he relocked the door of the cell. He said, "Go ahead. I'll follow you."

Gunderson grinned. "Careful, aren't you?"

Wyatt said simply, "It pays." He followed Gunderson into the office. He asked, "Where *is* your crew? I was just in the saloon and I didn't see them there. And they weren't in the hotel."

"They're probably down at the restaurant."

"All right. Go get them out of town."

"Sure, Matt. And thanks."

"All right. Just do what you said you'd do."

"Sure." Gunderson opened the door.

"And stay away from Doc."

"Doc? What would I want with him?"

"Same thing you wanted with Daisy. Stay away from him."

Gunderson shrugged. "You're the boss."

Wyatt watched Gunderson stride away up the street. He watched until Gunderson turned the corner at the hotel.

Then he closed the door and bolted it. He went back again to the cells. "Daisy?"

"What?"

"You want anything?"

"No, sir."

Wyatt looked at the four boys. "How about you? Need anything?"

Only Carl Eggers answered. "No, sir." The others stayed silent.

Leaving a lamp burning on the shelf at the end of the corridor, Wyatt returned to the office. The cigar was only half smoked, but it had gone out. He relighted it and again unlocked the door. He went out and sat on the bench beside the door.

A breeze blew from the south, warm with June, fragrant with blossoms of some kind in the creek bottom. Wyatt puffed idly on his cigar. Uptown, he heard a shout, and another . . . and, shortly after that, Gunderson strode around the corner beside the hotel, followed by his crew, all of them mounted. He led them to the Ace High Saloon and they all dismounted and trooped inside.

Disgustedly, Wyatt threw his cigar into the street. He got up, wincing as he put his weight on his injured leg. Gunderson had promised to get his crew out of town. Maybe he still would, after they'd had a drink or two, but that hadn't been part of the bargain.

He went back inside and closed the door. He bolted it, crossed to the couch, and sat down. He pulled off his boots and sailed his hat at the desk. With a groan, he laid back and closed his eyes. He was almost instantly asleep.

The Means brothers had spent most of the day making arrangements for Arnold's funeral. Later, they had helped Eggers guard the jail, and at suppertime had brought trays back for the prisoners, staying while Eggers went to eat. When Eggers returned, they went up to the hotel. They registered and immediately went up to their room.

Both men were shocked at what had happened to Arnold. Both were shocked at the way he had died. They'd had little in common with him, and had never been able to understand why he preferred a store in town to a ranch or farm, but he had been their brother, and they intended to see that his killers got what was coming to them.

At nine-thirty, there was a knock on their door. Bertram answered it and found Travis Williams, who was a partner in the Kiowa Mercantile Company, standing there. Williams said, "You two had better come over to the saloon."

"Why?"

"Gunderson and his crew are there, talking big. They claim those boys are going to get off."

"Going to get off? What do they know about it? The kids were just arrested today."

141

Williams shrugged. "I don't know how they know. But they claim when the thing comes to trial, there won't be enough evidence to convict."

Bertram looked at Lane. "I think we'd better go see what this is all about."

Lane nodded. He blew out the lamp and followed his brother out the door. The three went down the stairs, across the lobby, and into the street.

From the hotel veranda, they could plainly hear the noise from the saloon across the street. There must have been thirty horses tied out front, and to the hitch rails of adjoining stores. Bertram said, "I thought Gunderson was in jail. Wyatt must have let him go."

Williams said, "He did. Gunderson promised to take his crew and get out of town. But, after he got out, he said a couple of drinks wouldn't hurt."

Bertram strode angrily across the street, with Lane and Williams following. There was a big crowd in the saloon, and Gunderson's crew was only a part of it. Bertram stopped just inside the door, scowling at the scene, which was more like a celebration than anything else.

He saw Gunderson at the bar and angrily crossed the room toward him. He grabbed Gunderson by the shoulder and whirled him around. "What is this I hear? What is all this about my brother's killers getting off?"

Gunderson looked guilty, but only for an

instant. Dutch Hahn was standing beside him, and Hahn moved forward, as though to intervene. Gunderson shook his head at the foreman and Hahn stepped back. Gunderson said, "They probably will get off. They didn't mean to kill Arnold. It was an accident."

"Accident? He was kicked to death. The sheriff told me so himself."

Gunderson shook his head. "When something like this happens, everybody gets excited about it at first. Then they calm down. Now Doc says it was an accident. Your brother fell and hit his head."

"You are a liar! I saw him. I saw his body at McNiel's and I saw the bruises on his face and head."

Gunderson said placatingly, "You're upset, Mr. Means. After you've had time to cool off, you won't want those boys going to prison because of an accident any more than anybody else."

"I want justice for my brother. And I will see that justice is done."

"It's goin' to be up to the court, Mr. Means. It ain't goin' to be up to you."

"I suppose you've bought Daisy too," Bertram said bitterly.

"Nobody's bought anybody." There was an edge now to Gunderson's voice. "And I'd advise you not to go around makin' statements unless you're ready to back 'em up."

"I'll back them up." He turned and glanced

around the room. He raised his voice so that it carried over the noise. "A lot of you were Arnold's friends! A lot of you want to see justice done! I'd like to have those of you who cared about my brother to come up to the church! We will have a meeting! We will talk about what is to be done when the fathers of the criminals bribe and threaten witnesses!"

Dutch Hahn stepped forward and grabbed Bertram's arm. "Now wait a minute, you! You can't. . . ."

Gunderson said sharply, "Dutch!"

Dutch Hahn glanced around, and Gunderson shook his head at the man. Hahn released Bertram's arm.

Bertram strode toward the door, followed by Williams and his brother Lane. Twelve or fifteen other men, mostly town merchants, followed them. The group stopped just outside the saloon, and Bertram said, "I will go talk to the preacher and get the church opened up. The rest of you go around town and tell the rest of Arnold's friends that a meeting is to be held. Tell them what is happening. Tell them it is being arranged that Arnold's killers will get off."

The group dispersed, leaving Lane and Bertram alone. Lane said, "What about the sheriff? Want me to go get him?"

Bertram shook his head. "Leave him be."

Lane nodded. Bertram headed uptown toward the church, which was on the corner of Elm and B, across the street from the courthouse.

It was a two-block walk from the saloon, and it took only a few minutes for them to reach it. The church was dark, but there was light in the windows of the parsonage next door. Bertram knocked on the parsonage door and Mrs. Vaughn, the preacher's wife, answered it. She said, "Mr. Means! Come in! I'm so sorry about Arnold. He was such a fine man, and we all thought so much of him!"

Bertram said impatiently, "Yes, ma'am, Mrs. Vaughn. Will you tell your husband that we are here." He did not go inside.

She looked at him seeming puzzled for a moment, then said, "Of course," and withdrew. A few moments later Hiram Vaughn, the Methodist minister, came to the door. Bertram said, "We want to hold a meeting, preacher, and we want you to open up the church."

"A meeting? At this time of night?"

"A meeting of Arnold's friends." Bertram did not elaborate.

Vaughn doubtfully studied his face for a long moment. At last he nodded reluctantly. He came out the door and crossed the lawn to the church, followed by Bertram and Lane. A couple of men were already waiting at the door of the church, and several more were visible coming up the street. Vaughn went in and lighted a lamp that stood on a shelf beside the door. Bertram said, "Lane, light some more lamps."

Lane moved to obey. Vaughn stood at the door, studying the faces of the men who came through, his expression worried. He knew this was no meeting to mourn a dead friend.

He withdrew, and nobody even noticed that he had gone. He hurried along the street, heading for the jail.

CHAPTER

15

Nearly exhausted, Wyatt was already asleep when Vaughn pounded on the door. He swung his feet to the floor and sat there groggily for a moment, trying to gather his senses. He hadn't the slightest idea how long he had been asleep, but it was still dark.

He got up, nearly fell when his hurt leg gave, and staggered to the door. He peered out one of the windows to make sure no mob was waiting for him to open it. Seeing only one man, he unbolted it and swung it wide.

Hiram Vaughn stood on the walk. He said, "Sheriff? I've got to talk to you."

Wyatt stood aside. "All right. Come in."

He closed the door, then stumbled to his desk, where he lighted a lamp. He fumbled around in one of the desk cubbyholes until he found a cigar. Turning, he lighted it. "What's the trouble, Mr. Vaughn?"

"It's Bertram and Lane Means and some other men. They're having a meeting at the church."

"At this time of night?"

"Yes. That's what troubles me. They are all worked up, Sheriff, and I'm afraid they're planning trouble."

Wyatt said, "Damn!" He fumbled for his watch and looked at it. It was only ten-fifteen. He must have gotten all of an hour's sleep. He looked at Vaughn and asked, "I don't suppose you noticed whether Gunderson's crew was still in town when you came by the saloon."

Vaughn shook his head.

"All right, Mr. Vaughn. Go on back home. I'll come up to the church and see what's going on."

Vaughn was obviously relieved. "Thank you, Sheriff." He went to the door, turned, hesitated, then went out, closing it behind him.

Wyatt pulled on his boots. He got his hat from the desk and put it on. He ran a rueful hand over his face, feeling the stubble there. Hell, he hadn't even had time to shave today. Grumbling sourly, he blew out the lamp and went out. He locked the door behind him even though he wasn't worried about anyone trying to break the boys out of jail. Gunderson was capable of it, and Shapiro was capable of hiring it done, but neither man had reason to try it yet. They had bribed and threatened all the witnesses and had no need for force. As things stood now, the boys would get off, or draw nominal prison terms.

At the saloon, he stopped. He did not go in, but stood on the walk looking through the open doors. There was a fog of smoke in the place, and a steady roar of sound as if everybody was trying to talk at once. Wyatt didn't see Gunderson, but he saw Dutch Hahn and several members of Gunderson's crew. He cursed Gunderson beneath his breath for lying to him, then went on toward the church, limping very noticeably. The leg had stiffened even in the short time that he had slept, and it was even more painful now than it had been earlier.

He turned the corner at the hotel, walked the block to B Street, then headed toward the church. The church was on the corner. Next to it on the west was the parsonage, and next to that was Del Eggers' house.

Passing Eggers' house, in which there still were lights, Wyatt heard a movement on the porch. Josie came down the walk to the gate and called to him. "Matt? Is that you?"

"It's me."

"How is your leg?"

"Stiff."

"You shouldn't be walking on it."

He did not reply to that. She asked, "Were you looking for me? Or Pa?"

"Neither one. There's a meeting going on at the church. Hiram Vaughn got me out of bed to come break it up."

"A meeting? At this time of night?"

"Bertram and Lane Means and some of Arnold's friends."

"Why would they think it was necessary to meet in the middle of the night?"

"A lot has been going on. Sol Shapiro and Olaf

149

Gunderson have been trying to bribe the witnesses, and threatened them. I suppose Bertram and Lane figure they've got to fight back any way they can."

"What do you mean, any way they can? You don't think they'd try taking the law into their own hands, do you?"

"No. I don't mean that. I mean they might try to counter what Gunderson and Shapiro have done. They might try to reassure the witnesses, maybe even provide guards for them."

Josie was silent for a long time. At last Wyatt said, "Josie, I couldn't have done anything else. I had to arrest Carl. If it hadn't been me, it would have been somebody else."

"I know. And I don't blame you. But prison . . . maybe for the rest of his life. . . ."

"It probably won't be that bad." Privately, Matt was beginning to wonder if the boys would ever go to trial. If this much tension could build up in a single day, it was more than likely that things would erupt in violence before the case ever went to trial.

"What . . . what if he was to escape?"

"He wouldn't get very far. Don't think about it, Josie. It's no use."

"But suppose he did? And suppose he got away?"

"He'd be a fugitive. He'd spend his whole life wondering when someone was going to tap him on the shoulder and take him away."

"Would that be worse than spending his whole

life behind bars?" she asked bitterly.

"Maybe not, but it's impossible."

"Is it, Matt? Is it?"

He knew what she was getting at. She hadn't asked him yet, but he had a feeling that, sooner or later, she would. He said, "Josie, I've got to go."

"Of course, Matt. Good night." There was now a discernible coolness in her voice, and he frowned as he walked away. He couldn't blame her for thinking along the lines of escape for Carl. But he hoped she wasn't going to try to pressure him. He didn't want to have to refuse her a thing like that.

He passed the parsonage. There were no horses tied in front of the church, and the doors and windows all were closed so that no noise escaped the place. Only the lighted windows betrayed the fact that anyone was inside.

Hiram Vaughn was waiting for him on the steps of the church. Wyatt said, "I thought you were going home."

"I wouldn't be able to sleep. I'd lie there wondering what was going on. Would it be all right if I came in?"

"I don't see why not. It's your church." He opened the door and stepped inside. Vaughn stepped in immediately behind.

There were more than thirty men in the room. They were clustered down by the pulpit. Bertram Means stood in the pulpit, facing them. His face was red, his anger visible even from in the back of the church. Wyatt slid into one of the back pews and made room for Vaughn to sit beside him. He whispered, "Let's see what they're talking about."

Bertram was saying, ". . . and Gunderson threatened her. Sam Purdue says that he saw Wyatt arrest him when he was comin' out of her house. He arrested Daisy later and put her in jail. Got a warrant from the judge charging her with prostitution, but it was just a dodge to put her where Gunderson and Shapiro couldn't get to her."

Someone yelled, "What difference could that make? The damage has already been done. Daisy won't point the finger at a single one of them boys now. Unless it would be Carl and Frank. You can bet Orvie and Marv are goin' to get off."

"That's what we're here to talk about. I don't intend to see this thing rigged so that they do get off. Arnold was too good a man to die in an alley like that, and then have his killers get away with it."

"Sure, but what can we do? Shapiro's even got Doc scared. Threatened not to renew the mortgage on his house."

Wyatt got to his feet. He didn't see how Bertram Means could have come by that piece of information. He yelled, "Who told you that?"

Another man stood up. Wyatt recognized him as the newspaperman from Kansas City, who had gotten off the train today, and who he'd talked to in the hotel dining room. "I told him, Sheriff."

"And who told you?"

"I talked to Doctor McNab. I got the information straight from him."

Wyatt cursed beneath his breath, then glanced apologetically at Vaughn. He stepped past Vaughn into the aisle and walked toward the front. Bertram glared angrily at him. "What are you going to do about it, Sheriff?"

"Do?" Wyatt was suddenly almost as angry as Bertram. "What the hell do you expect me to do? I've arrested all four of the boys. I've got Daisy in protective custody. What more can I do?"

"You didn't have to let Gunderson loose."

"He promised to take his crew and get out of town. That's why I let him go."

"But he didn't take 'em out of town. He's down at the saloon right now, bragging and throwing his weight around. It's like a celebration down there. And Arnold ain't even buried yet."

Wearily Wyatt said, "You men go home. You're only going to make things worse."

Bertram said, "We're not going home. We're staying until we decide what we're going to do."

"You'd better not do anything. I'll throw you in jail just as quickly as I did those boys."

"But not Sol Shapiro! Not the man who threatened Doc and tried to make him change the story he'd tell in court. Not Gunderson, either! Not the one who scared Daisy so bad she can't be counted on to say anything but what he told her to."

"Who told you that?"

"Nobody had to tell us. We know Gunderson. He didn't make no social call on Daisy today. If he went to see her, it was to threaten her, or to bribe her, or both. Otherwise, he wouldn't be down at the saloon celebrating now. Not with his kid in jail, charged with murder!"

Wyatt wished Ralph Griffin, the newspaperman, had stayed out of it. Or that Doc had had sense enough to keep his mouth shut. But Griffin hadn't stayed out of it, and Doc had blabbed, and now these men knew the whole story, even though they weren't absolutely sure of their facts.

They suspected what he did, that the trial was going to end up a farce, with all four of the boys getting off practically scot free, or with Carl and Frank taking the blame for all four and paying the penalty.

Bertram, even more red of face than before, roared, "I tell you for myself, Sheriff, and for my brother too! We ain't going to let those dirty killers get away with what they done. If the law lets them go, then we're going to execute them ourselves!"

A roar of approval went up from the assembled men. Griffin had a faint smile on his face. He was a troublemaker, Wyatt thought. A murder story wasn't big enough for him. He had to make it bigger if he could. And if inciting these men to violence would make it bigger, then he'd do that.

Wyatt shouted, "All of you go home!" The roar scarcely quieted at all. He shouted again, "Go home! I'm ordering you to go home!"

Someone shouted, "Or you'll do what? Throw us all in jail with those murderers? Maybe we ought to let you throw us all in jail! Maybe then we'd see that justice was done ourselves!"

Some members of the crowd laughed at that, but there was no humor in their laughs. Wyatt glanced at the minister. Vaughn nodded and got up in the pulpit beside Bertram Means. He raised both hands for quiet, and, out of respect, the crowd quieted. Vaughn said reprovingly, "This is the house of God!"

Someone yelled, "I reckon God is as interested as we are in seeing killers punished for what they done!"

"No one has said these boys will not be punished, if they are proven guilty!"

"What do you mean, *if!*"

"The law says they are innocent until proven guilty," Vaughn said stiffly.

"How the hell are they goin' to be proven guilty if their fathers bribe and threaten the witnesses?"

Vaughn looked helpless a moment. He hesitated between supporting his statement and reproving the man who had used the word hell. He finally said, as stiffly and as ineffectively as before, "Justice will prevail!"

A man bawled, "You're damned right it will. Even if we have to make sure of it ourselves!"

CHAPTER

16

Bertram raised both hands for quiet. He yelled, "We ain't going home, and we ain't going to be arrested. Let's get on with this. Let's decide what we're goin' to do!"

And now, the suggestion Wyatt had been waiting for came from someone in the back, "Let's string 'em up!"

It had a certain shock value, that for an instant caused a silence in the room. Vaughn stepped into the breech, bawling in his best pulpit voice, "Shame on all of you! To suggest such a thing in the house of God!"

Bertram said, "Quiet, Preacher." Raising his voice, he yelled, "Maybe we'll come to that! But right now, I think it's too soon. Anybody got any other ideas?"

Someone shouted, "How about a run on Shapiro's bank, starting first thing in the morning? We could start it, and then tell him that unless he backs off, and lets the law take its course, we're going to break him *and* his bank!"

There was a chorus of approving shouts.

Wyatt stepped up beside Bertram Means. He raised his hands, palms out to quiet them. He said, "I've got a better idea. If you're all willing to put your money where your mouths are."

Angry grumbling answered him, but Bertram was interested. "What *is* your idea?"

Wyatt said, "Shapiro scared Doc by threatening not to renew his mortgage. Doc knew that if Shapiro didn't, he'd lose his house. What I suggest is that you each pledge a part of what Doc owes. Then Shapiro won't have any hold on him. Doc could say whatever he wanted to in court, without being afraid of the consequences."

A man yelled, "What about Daisy?"

Wyatt answered, "I think I can promise that Daisy will tell the truth. I've got her in jail where she'll be safe."

Someone yelled, "All right. I got seventy dollars I can spare! Put me down for that."

Bertram glanced at Hiram Vaughn. "Mind writing all this down for us?"

"I'll be happy to." Vaughn got paper and a pencil. He wrote down the first volunteer's name, and after it, $70.00.

There was a chorus of yelling voices in the room. Bertram called, "Line up. Give the preacher your names and the amount." Turning his head, he said, "Put Lane and me down for two hundred."

Vaughn wrote their names and the amount. A line had formed, and as each man reached the pulpit, he gave Vaughn his name and an amount. Largest single pledge was seventy-five dollars. Smallest was ten. Finished, Vaughn totaled the column and said, "It comes to nine hundred eighty-six dollars. Anybody know how big the mortgage is?"

Nobody did. Wyatt said, "I'll go talk to Doc. I'll tell him what's happened, and what you've all agreed to do." Looking at Vaughn he said, "Mind giving me that list?"

Vaughn handed it to him. Wyatt said, "Go home now. All of you."

Bertram said, "If you don't mind, Lane and me will help you watch the jail."

Wyatt shrugged. The crowd began to disperse, filing out of the church, talking quietly among themselves. The excitement and anger seemed to be gone from them, temporarily, anyway, but Wyatt knew it would return if there appeared to be any further chance the four boys were going to get away with what they had done.

When all the men had gone, Vaughn blew out the lamps, then closed and locked the door. He said good night and headed for the parsonage. Bertram said, "We'll go with you."

"All right. Let's go." Wyatt wished that he had cautioned all the men not to say anything about what had been decided. A few of them were bound to go to the saloon for a drink before going home, and someone might let something slip.

But it was too late now. He headed down Elm

Street toward Doc McNab's, accompanied by Bertram Means and Lane.

Lamps still burned inside Doc's house. Wyatt went up on the porch and knocked. Mrs. McNab answered the door. Wyatt said, "We'd like to talk to Doc."

"Can't it wait until morning, Sheriff?"

He shook his head. "I'm afraid it can't."

"All right. Come in." She stood aside, a slight frown upon her face.

Wyatt went in, followed by Bertram and Lane. The three stood in the parlor, holding their hats in their hands. Mrs. McNab left the room, and a few moments later Doc appeared.

Wyatt said, "Doc, I know that Sol Shapiro threatened you. But some of Arnold's friends got together over at the church tonight, and they all pledged to help you out when your mortgage at the bank comes due. I don't know how much it is, but this is how much was pledged, and the name of each man that agreed to help." He handed the list to Doc.

Doc took it, his hands trembling. He stared down at it for a long, long time, so long, in fact, that Wyatt began to wonder if he was ever going to look up. He did, at last, and there were tears in his eyes. He looked at Wyatt for a moment, then forced himself to look at Bertram and at Lane. He looked away, then, determinedly, looked back at them again. "I am ashamed. I don't think I would have done it, but I don't know for sure."

Wyatt asked, "How much is your mortgage,

Doc? Is that enough?"

"It is almost enough. I will be able to make up the rest myself."

"Then you've got nothing to worry about. You can tell the truth about Arnold's death."

"I can. And I will. You can depend on me."

Wyatt looked at Bertram Means. "Let's go." There was an urgency in his voice that made Bertram glance quickly at his face. Wyatt said good night to Doc and went out, followed by Bertram and Lane. He heard the door close behind them and said, "Let's get back down to the jail."

"Why? What's the rush?"

"Nobody's there. I let Del Eggers go on home."

"So what? You locked the door, didn't you?"

"Sure I locked the door. But some of the men who met at the church might have gone by the saloon for a drink on their way home. They might have let something slip."

"And you think that if Gunderson and Shapiro knew Doc was going to tell the truth, they might try breaking those kids out of jail?"

"I don't think they would. But I think they might. So I'd just as soon get back."

The three hurried down the east side of the street, past Shapiro's bank, and past the hotel across the street from it. Wyatt could see no one between the saloon and the jail. The street was deserted, but the noise continued inside the saloon. Bertram growled angrily, "The bastards!

It's like they were celebrating!"

They crossed Longhorn Street. The jail lay ahead, a faint light glowing inside from the single lamp Wyatt had left burning. The padlock on the door was intact. He unlocked it, then locked it again in the hasp. He opened the door.

Bertram came in behind him, gun drawn. Lane stayed outside for an instant.

But there was no cause for alarm. Everything was quiet inside the jail. Wyatt went to the rear of the office and opened the door leading to the cells. The lamp was smoking on the shelf at the end of the corridor. He walked back to it and trimmed the wick.

Orvie and Marv were lying on the cots in one of the cells, Frank Avila and Carl Eggers on the cots in the other one. Wyatt opened the door that had been built into the new partition and glanced at Daisy. She was asleep on the cot in her cell, the blanket pulled up to her chin.

The four boys appeared to be asleep, but Wyatt suspected they were feigning it. He went back into the office and closed the door. He said, "All quiet back there." He stared at Bertram a moment, then crossed the room and bolted the outside door. He said, "I was rousted out of bed at one o'clock this morning. If you don't mind, I'm going to get some sleep."

Bertram and Lane settled themselves as comfortably as they could. Bertram sat at the sheriff's desk. Lane sat in a straight-backed chair, which he tipped back against the wall. Almost immediately, the sheriff began to snore.

Silence lay over the room for a long time. At last Lane said softly, "Don't seem possible."

"What don't?"

"That Arnold's dead. I always figured, if any of us got hurt or killed, it would be you or me. But not Arnold. He was too quiet, and all he ever wanted was to run that store. I guess we got to be kind of proud of him."

"Proud, hell. What he done was stupid. She's only a whore, an' them kids wouldn't have done nothing to her that hadn't been done before."

Lane was silent a moment. Then he looked up, a bit of defiance in his eyes. "I still think Arnold done what was right. Any woman's got the right to say no when she wants to. Even a whore."

Bertram did not take up the argument. They sat in silence for a long time. Wyatt's snoring grew louder, then stopped, then began again. Bertram stared across the room at him. "He's a damn good man. I don't blame him for being tired. He got them four boys all by himself."

"He's liable to have trouble with that pitchfork wound. Them things can be mean, especially if the fork's dirty."

"If it was in Gunderson's barn, it was dirty all right."

"The women will be worried."

"No they won't. They know why we stayed in town. One of us can ride out there in the morning."

"What do you reckon Gunderson's goin' to do?"

"He'll do his damndest to get his kid out of it. Anybody would."

"Would you? If it was one of your kids?"

"I don't know. I guess I would."

"Even if you knew they'd done it?"

Bertram hesitated for a time. At last he said, almost reluctantly, "Even then."

"What do you think Gunderson and Shapiro will do when they know we got up the money for Doc?"

Bertram frowned. "They won't give up. That's for sure."

"You think they'll try to break them kids out of jail?"

"They might."

Lane was silent for a time. At last he said worriedly, "Three of us ain't very many to hold this jail if Gunderson and his crew was to take a notion to break into it."

"Maybe not."

"You think one of us ought to go up to the saloon and see what's goin' on?"

Bertram glanced at Wyatt, who was still snoring softly, his mouth open. He said, "Maybe."

"You want me to go?"

"Sure. Go ahead." He looked at the wall clock. "They won't be closin' for a couple of hours yet."

"Don't seem possible all this started just last night."

163

"No, it doesn't. Bring back a bottle when you come. It's liable to be a damn long night."

"Sure." Lane got up and went to the door. Bertram followed him. Lane opened it and peered outside. "Don't see anybody in the street."

"Knock three times when you come back. And don't be gone too long. The sheriff might wake up."

"All right. I'll hurry." Lane went out. Bertram watched him walk up the street for a little way. Then he closed the door and bolted it again.

He went back and sat down at the desk. He filled and packed his pipe. He lighted it and puffed thoughtfully.

His initial anger over Arnold's death had cooled, but his determination to see the killers punished had not lessened. Now he asked himself what he would do if Gunderson and his men did storm the jail. He wondered if he could shoot into them.

Frowning, he shook his head. No man could make that decision beforehand. No man could decide ahead of time what he would do when the time for action came.

He got up and began pacing nervously back and forth, wishing Lane would return.

CHAPTER

17

Olaf Gunderson had been jubilant when he left the jail. And while he had promised Wyatt he would take his crew and get out of town, he didn't see what harm a few drinks would do. He'd had a damn rough day, beginning when Wyatt came riding out to the ranch accusing Orvie of the murder of Arnold Means. He'd been knocked out, arrested, thrown in jail, and finally released. He'd had the hell scared out of him by the thought of Orvie hanging for the crime. If anyone had ever needed a drink, he needed one. So instead of going straight out to the ranch, he'd come to the saloon.

The crew, led by Dutch Hahn, took their mood from him. They were noisy and jubilant, as though this was a celebration, as though Arnold Means did not lie unburied up at the undertaking establishment, his body scarcely cold.

Contemplating his drink, Gunderson wondered what kind of sentence Orvie would actually get when the case went to court. He was sure

Daisy would testify that Orvie hadn't touched Arnold Means, and that would help. Doc would testify that Arnold's death might have been caused accidentally, and Brock Davidson would testify that Daisy often turned a trick on the side, and that she might have gone into the alley of her own free will. Hell, the kids might get off scot free, at least Marv Shapiro and Orvie might. The other two would get no more than an assault conviction, and a year or two in prison.

But damn Orvie! He was going to catch hell when he got out of jail. Olaf didn't intend to go through this sort of thing again.

Several men came into the saloon. They were townsmen, mostly businessmen. They frowned disapprovingly at Gunderson and at his boisterous crew.

Olaf knew they were friends of Arnold Means. He knew they disapproved of the air of celebration in the saloon. Maybe, he thought, he ought to take his crew and go on home, the way he'd promised Matt.

The townsmen went to the bar, taking a place at the end that was, for the moment, unoccupied.

Olaf spoke to Dutch, standing next to him. "Tell the boys to finish their drinks. We'll be leaving in ten or fifteen minutes."

"Sure, boss." Dutch left him and began circulating among the men.

Olaf glanced again at the townsmen, his glance drawn, perhaps, by the attention they were giving him. As if he was glad Arnold Means was dead. As if he was some kind of monster who didn't even care.

Well, he did care. He'd known Arnold himself. He'd traded with him. He had liked the man.

But when it came to a man's own son . . . well the ties of blood were strong, particularly since Orvie was his only son. Nothing else mattered. He'd do anything he had to do for Orvie, with no regrets, however often he had wished Orvie was different.

What made a boy so violent, he wondered now. What made him beat animals in a kind of crazy frenzy until he was stopped physically? What had made him kick Arnold Means in the head last night, long after he was unconscious? For Olaf had little doubt it had been Orvie who had administered the kick that had actually killed Arnold Means.

Would Orvie change as the years passed? He shook his head, lifted his drink, and gulped it down. He glanced at Brock. "Add it up," he said, and shoved a twenty-dollar gold piece across the bar.

Brock figured a few minutes, then made change. Olaf looked around for Dutch. The man was coming toward him from the other end of the bar, accompanied by a crippled-up horse wrangler named Horne. Olaf paid little attention to the pair, still thinking about his son.

He doubted if Orvie would ever change. But the damn kid was going to have to learn to control himself. This was the first serious scrape he'd been in, but, if he didn't curb his temper, it wouldn't be the last. And next time his father might not be able to get him out of it.

Dutch said, "Boss, Pop Horne overheard some of what them townsmen were sayin' down at the end of the bar."

"And what was that?" Olaf looked at Horne.

The man cleared his throat. He was only in his middle forties, but he looked more than sixty. He'd ridden so many bucking broncs that his insides were scrambled up like eggs. He limped when he walked, and he hated to ride a horse because it hurt. Pop Horne said, "Well, Mr. Gunderson, they're sayin' that they got up the money to pay off the mortgage on Doc McNab's house. They're sayin' that now Doc will tell the truth in court, and that Orvie an' them other boys will hang."

Olaf felt as if he had been kicked in the belly by a mule. If Doc told the truth, then Daisy, who was being held in jail, and couldn't be reached again, might also tell the truth. Her story, and Doc's, would be enough to convict the boys, no matter what Brock Davidson might have to say.

He knew his face must look as pale as it felt. He said, "Take the boys out toward the ranch, Dutch, but don't take 'em all the way. Pull off the road and stop out there where the road crosses that dry wash. Wait for me."

"Sure, boss." Dutch didn't question him. Olaf was suddenly glad Dutch was so dependable.

The man would do anything for him, even go to jail, he supposed. The crew would be there when he wanted them, and it was beginning to look as though he was going to want them yet tonight.

He watched them leave, quieted now, as though they sensed trouble in the air. There was a brief commotion outside as they untied their horses, mounted, and rode down the street and out of town.

Gunderson poured himself one last drink. The townsmen finished their drinks and left. There were still half a dozen men in the saloon, but Sol Shapiro wasn't one of them.

Olaf gulped his drink, nodded shortly at Brock, and went outside. He stood in front until all the townsmen had disappeared, heading separately toward their homes. He glanced down the street, but, because of the darkness, he didn't see Lane Means coming toward him from the jail.

He untied his horse and mounted. He turned the corner on Texas Street and headed west. At G Street he turned north again and rode straight to Sol Shapiro's house.

There still were lights in the house, though it was well past the time when Sol and his wife usually went to bed. He tied his horse to the hitching post in front of the Shapiro house and went up the walk.

Sol must have heard him, because the door opened before he reached the porch. Sol's shirt was open at the neck. His hair was mussed, and he looked distraught. Olaf said, "I've got to talk to you."

"Maybe I'd better come on out. Minnie is practically hysterical."

"Then you'd better come on out."

Sol closed the door and came out onto the porch. He walked toward the street, with Gunderson following. At the gate, Shapiro stopped. "Well?"

"A bunch of townsmen, friends of Arnold's, got together at the church tonight. All of them pledged money to help Doc pay his mortgage off. So you ain't got the hold on him you thought you had."

In the darkness he couldn't see Shapiro's face, but, from past experience with the man he could imagine the look on it. If this hadn't been so serious, he would have grinned with enjoyment, thinking about it. There was a long silence. Any other man would have cursed, but not Solomon Shapiro. At last he asked, "So what are we going to do?"

"Well, I don't know what you're going to do, but I'm not going to let my boy go to trial. Doc's story won't help either of them, and if Doc tells the truth, the chances are Daisy will too. Those boys could hang. Arnold Means was a well-liked man, and the jury is going to be chosen from friends of his."

"How can you keep them from going to trial? Do you mean to say you're going to break them out of jail?"

"That's exactly what I mean."

"You'll go to jail yourself."

"Maybe. But I won't hang."

"Where will they go after you get them out of jail? They'll be outlaws. They'll be wanted men, and they're only fifteen years old."

"It's better than being dead, ain't it?"

"Maybe they wouldn't hang. Maybe they'd only go to prison."

"Is that any better? Spending their lives in prison?"

"I guess not," Shapiro said reluctantly.

"Are you going to help?"

"What can *I* do?"

Gunderson stared at him in the near darkness for a long time. He didn't like Sol Shapiro, and never had. Shapiro was a miser. All he cared about was money, and he had a lot of it. Gunderson said brutally, "You can get your hands dirty along with me for a change. If you don't, I'll just leave Marv in jail."

"What if I *do* help?"

"Well, I guess between us we've got enough money to get them to Mexico."

"And what can they do there?"

Gunderson said sourly, "If Marv is anything like you, he'll own the damn place in a year or two."

"This is no time for jokes," Sol reproved him humorlessly.

"Maybe not. The point I was trying to make is that we got enough money to keep the kids in

Mexico, even if they can't get jobs."

"How will they get to Mexico?"

"You leave that to me. I'll send Dutch Hahn and three or four men along with them. Dutch has come up the trail with a cattle herd five or six times, and he knows every ranch and soddy between here and Paso Del Norte."

Sol asked, "When will you break them out?"

"Tonight. As soon as I can get things organized."

"Nobody will get hurt?"

"I hope not."

"What do you mean, you hope not? If anybody else gets killed, we'll all go on trial."

Gunderson felt his anger flare. He said savagely, "You son-of-a-bitch, what do you want, a guarantee? You want to be sure it's safe? Well, it ain't safe. One of us might get killed, and someone in the jail might get killed. That's the chance we got to take."

Shapiro wilted. "What about the other boys? You going to get them out and send them to Mexico along with Orvie and Marv?"

"I don't know," Gunderson growled. "I haven't decided yet."

"What do you want me to do?"

"Give Minnie some excuse. Get away from the house and meet me in an hour down by the depot. And bring a gun."

"I'll have to stop by the bank. I keep a shotgun there."

"All right, do it," Gunderson said impatiently.

172

He started away, but turned as he reached his horse. "An hour. If you're not there, Marv can rot in jail for all I care."

"I'll be there." Shapiro's voice was tight and scared.

Gunderson untied his horse and mounted. He rode down the street at a walk, his own nerves drawn tight. He didn't want to attract attention now.

He began to plan as he rode. Wyatt would be at the jail. Eggers had gone home. Bertram and Lane Means might also be at the jail.

Wyatt was sensible. He wouldn't go for his gun if doing so would only get him shot. He'd wait, get up a posse, and come after Orvie and Marv tomorrow.

But Gunderson wasn't sure about Bertram and Lane. They'd lost their brother, and they were angry. If they thought his killers were going to get away, they might be tempted to do something foolish.

He'd just have to plan it so they didn't get the chance. He reached the lower end of town. His horse picked his way across the railroad tracks and finally struck the road that led out to his ranch south of town.

Only then did he lift his horse to a lope. At this gait, he reached the bridge across the dry wash in fifteen minutes more.

Dutch was waiting beside the road. The crew was nowhere to be seen. Dutch said, "They're back off the road about a quarter mile. I figured the Means brothers might be comin' home, and I didn't want them to be seen."

"Go get them."

"Yes, sir. What are we goin' to do?"

"We're going to get Orvie out of jail. I want you to pick three or four of the men, and I want you to take Orvie and Marv Shapiro to Mexico. Matt Wyatt will be coming after you, but I figure you can get away from him all right. Particularly if you've got five or six hours' start."

"Don't worry, boss. I won't get caught."

"All right. Get the men and we'll get at it. But tell 'em I want no shooting unless it's absolutely necessary. Anyone who does anything foolish will answer to the law himself, without any help from me."

"I'll tell 'em, boss." Dutch rode away, disappearing almost immediately. Gunderson waited impatiently for him to return.

CHAPTER

18

Lane Means, approaching from the direction of the jail, and hidden by shadows, saw Gunderson's crew leave the saloon. He halted, stepped into a doorway, and watched as they rode their horses past, heading south toward home. He remained in the doorway until the last of them had disappeared.

Scrutinizing them carefully as they passed, he had failed to see Olaf Gunderson with them, and this puzzled him. It puzzled him enough to hold him there, motionless, for several minutes more.

He saw several townsmen come from the saloon, saw them straggle away toward their homes. Still waiting, he saw Gunderson come out, saw him pause and watch the disappearing townsmen. Gunderson then untied his horse and mounted him. But instead of following his crew toward home, he turned north and rounded the corner of Texas Street, heading west.

His curiosity aroused, Lane broke into a fast walk. He passed the saloon, reached the corner, and stopped just short of it. Peering around, he saw Gunderson just turning the corner of Texas and G, this time going north.

Gunderson had to be heading for Sol Shapiro's house, he guessed. But why, at this time of night? What was urgent enough to take him to Shapiro's, well after the banker's bedtime?

He broke into a trot, and rounding the second corner, saw Gunderson's horse tied to the hitch post in front of Shapiro's house. Lights were still burning in the house. Hurrying, Lane headed toward it. Something was up. He felt it, and he wanted to know what it was.

Well short of Shapiro's house, he left the gravel walk and cut across the lawns of the houses adjoining it. He approached Shapiro's porch from behind a screen of bushes and trees.

He almost gave himself away and stepped into sight. Barely in time, he heard the sound of voices. He stopped, hidden by a bush, and listened.

He heard Shapiro say, "You'll go to jail yourself," and immediately after heard Gunderson reply, "Maybe. But I won't hang at least."

Silent, his breathing quieted, Lane stood there listening. He heard them talking about breaking Orvie Gunderson and Marv Shapiro out of jail. He heard them planning to send the boys to Mexico, accompanied by Dutch Hahn and several reliable members of Gunderson's crew.

The break was to take place tonight. Gunderson would go immediately and get his crew. Shapiro would go to the bank and get a gun.

Though his sense of urgency was almost over-powering, Means waited until Olaf Gunderson untied his horse, mounted, and rode back down the street. He waited until Shapiro went back inside the house. The two had agreed to meet in an hour. He had forty-five minutes to do something about stopping them.

When Shapiro's door had closed, Lane turned and hurried down the street. The saloon was still open when he passed, but no noise came from it. Looking in, he saw Brock Davidson behind the bar. It didn't seem possible that Arnold had been killed about this time last night.

He went on to the jail and knocked lightly three times.

The door opened. Inside the jail it was dark. Lane went in. Bertram closed the door and bolted it. He asked, "Where's the bottle I told you to get?"

"I didn't go into the saloon."

"Why not?"

"Well, Gunderson's crew left the saloon right after I left here. They rode out of town, but Olaf Gunderson didn't go with them. I waited, and he finally came out, but instead of following them, he headed the other way. So I went after him."

"Where'd he go?"

"To Sol Shapiro's house. I sneaked up and listened. They were out in front talking. They were talking about breaking those kids out of here.

Tonight. Gunderson went to get his crew. Shapiro said he'd go down to the bank and get a gun. They're supposed to meet at the depot in an hour. Then they're coming here."

"They must have found out what we did tonight about Doc."

"Looks like it. A bunch of the men who were at the church left the saloon right after Gunderson's crew pulled out. They probably blabbed before they left."

Bertram cursed softly. Lane said, "You'd better wake Matt."

Bertram crossed the room to Wyatt's cot. The sheriff lay on his back, snoring softly. Bertram said, "Matt, wake up."

Wyatt came awake like an animal, with no start, with no sudden movement. His eyes opened, but otherwise he didn't stir. He said, "What do you want?"

"You'd better get up."

"Is something wrong?" Wyatt swung his feet to the floor and sat up on the cot. It creaked with his shift of weight. When his injured leg bent, he drew in his breath quickly, but otherwise gave no indication how much it hurt.

Bertram said, "Lane overheard Gunderson and Shapiro talking about breaking those boys out of jail. They're going to meet at the depot in an hour. Then they're coming here."

Wyatt got to his feet. The cot creaked again. Limping painfully, he walked to the window and stared into the street. He was silent for a long,

long time. This was what he had feared might happen when Gunderson and Shapiro realized that their efforts to bribe and intimidate the witnesses had failed.

Now a decision faced him, but he didn't want to make it hastily. Too much was involved. He could try getting along with only Bertram and Lane. Or he could send them out for help.

Bertram said, "We're going to need some help."

Wyatt nodded, his decision made. "All right. Round up fifteen or twenty men. Tell 'em to meet here, but tell 'em to keep out of sight and come here by way of the alley out in back."

He opened the door. Bertram and Lane went out. Trying to hold the jail with only Lane and Bertram to help would be foolish. Wyatt had known that almost instantly. They were personally involved. They could not be counted on to act dispassionately or with restraint.

Forewarned, he might be able to avert a crisis tonight. But what about tomorrow? And the day after that?

Sourly, he cursed beneath his breath. He wondered how quickly he could get Judge Whelan to hold the trial. The sooner it was all over with, the better for everyone. And there was no reason to delay. The boys were in jail, and the witnesses available to testify.

But tomorrow would take care of itself. It was tonight that worried him now. Gunderson was tough, and so was Hahn. Gunderson's crew was fanatically loyal. They'd do anything Gunderson told them to.

He suspected, furthermore, that Gunderson would notify Del Eggers what was happening, and get his help. He'd also notify Mrs. Avila, who in turn would round up as many of Frank's friends as possible. It could turn into quite a fight.

He began to pace nervously back and forth, gritting his teeth against the pain. He might need the use of his leg before the night was over with, and he ought to give it a chance to limber up.

The first man arrived less than fifteen minutes after Bertram and Lane had left. He knocked softly on the door and Wyatt admitted him. It was Galen Hobbs, who owned the livery barn. He was out of breath. He said, "I came as quick as I could. I got a ten-gauge shotgun. Is that all right?"

"Yeah. It's all right. I suppose all the shells you have are loaded with number six."

"Uh-huh."

Wyatt crossed the room. Out of a drawer beneath the gunrack he got a box of shells that were loaded with buckshot. He brought a handful of them back to Hobbs, who pocketed them silently.

Wyatt said, "I don't want to be caught by surprise. Will you go down to the depot and wait? Keep out of sight. When they all get there, you come back here and let me know."

"Sure." Hobbs went out, his shotgun clutched

tightly in his hand.

Wyatt stepped outside the door. The night air had turned chill. He shivered, and felt goose flesh raise on his arms. He hoped Gunderson wouldn't bring Del Eggers into this. Or he hoped that if Eggers was asked he would refuse.

Overhead, the stars were bright. An elusive fragrance was in the air, the same one he had smelled earlier. It must come from something blooming in the creek bottom, he thought, but it made him think of Josie Eggers. Thinking of her, he felt worse than ever about having her brother here in jail.

A man stepped around the corner of the jail, startling him, making him grab, with pure reflex, for his gun. Seeing who it was, he let his hand drop away from the gun grips self-consciously. He said softly, "Go on in the jail. Anybody come with you?"

The man was Jonas Hamilton, the saddlemaker. He said, "My boy's with me."

His "boy" was twenty-five. He worked with his father in the saddle shop. Hamilton called to him. Both of them then went into the jail.

Wyatt followed, bolting the door behind him. Hamilton had a rifle, but his son did not. Wyatt got him one from the rack and gave him some shells for it. He said, "Sit down and take it easy. Nothing's going to happen for a while."

Hamilton was plainly nervous. "You don't think it will come to a fight, do you?"

"It could."

Hamilton said, "I never shot at a man. I don't know. . . ."

"Maybe you won't have to." Wyatt opened the door that led to the cells in the rear. The lamp was still burning dimly on the shelf in the corridor. He looked in at the boys. Orvie Gunderson was asleep, snoring loudly. Marv Shapiro was lying down, but Wyatt could see his eyes gleam in the light from the lamp. Eggers and Frank Avila were sitting up on their cots, talking between themselves. Avila asked, "What's going on?"

"There may be a try at breaking you out of jail."

"They ain't figurin' on lynchin' us?" Avila's voice was scared.

"No. It's Gunderson and Shapiro. They're going to try and get you out and send you to Mexico."

Behind the partition he heard Daisy's quickly in-drawn breath. There was a silence, and then she called, "Mr. Wyatt?"

He opened the door in the partition and glanced at her. She was standing beneath the window, only faintly visible in the light thrown into her cell by the lamp in the corridor. Wyatt asked, "What do you want?"

"They'll kill me, sheriff. When they take those boys, they'll kill me, and say it was an accident."

"Nobody's going to be killing anyone. And nobody's taking the boys out of here." He glanced at the window above her head. Her fear of being killed was justified. She was the chief witness against the boys. Gunderson wouldn't hesitate to kill her if it would help get Orvie off. He said, "Move your cot over underneath the window."

"You think they might try shooting me through the window?"

"No. I don't think so. But it's possible. No harm in playing safe."

She quickly dragged her cot over beneath the window. She sat down on it and looked fearfully over her shoulder at the window above her head. It had glass in it. The bars were outside the glass. The wall was more than six inches thick. Wyatt doubted if anyone could shoot Daisy in her cot beneath the window, even if he had a ladder to climb up on. He said, "If you should hear the glass break, roll over close to the wall."

She moved quickly to put her back against the wall. Wyatt shut the partition door and returned to the office, closing that door after him. He heard the boys talking excitedly behind it, but the thickness of the door prevented him from making out what was being said.

Someone was knocking on the outside door. He crossed the room and opened it. There were perhaps a dozen men outside. Bertram Means was one of them. Wyatt said, "Come on in, all of you, and I'll tell you what has to be done."

They crowded in, subdued, talking softly among themselves. When they were all inside, Wyatt said, "Have you all got guns?"

183

Most signified assent. Three said that they did not. Wyatt got three guns from the rack, and gave each man the proper shells. Then he said, "I suppose you already know. Gunderson and Shapiro are going to try breaking the boys out of jail. I intend to stop them, but I want to avoid shooting if possible. So don't get trigger happy. Don't anybody shoot unless I give the order. Is that understood?"

A murmur of agreement went around the room.

Wyatt said, "All right then. Go on outside. Station yourselves where you can look down into the street, roof tops, upstairs windows, stairways, passageways between buildings, anyplace where you can see without being seen."

Silently the men crowded out of the room. Once in the street, they dispersed rapidly, with little talk.

Wyatt suddenly felt like a commander laying out his strategy for an impending battle. He fervently hoped that it wasn't going to come to that.

CHAPTER

19

Dutch Hahn was gone no more than a few minutes. When he returned, the entire Gunderson crew was with him. He hauled his horse to a halt in front of Gunderson and said, "What about them other two kids, boss? Carl Eggers and Frank Avila? You goin' to leave them in jail?"

Gunderson hesitated. The other two *were* Orvie's friends, and they were probably less guilty than Orvie was. Left in the jail, they'd end up paying the penalty for all four, probably a much more severe penalty than if all four had gone on trial together. He said, "All right, they can come out with Orvie and Marv. They can go to Mexico, too, if that's what they want."

Dutch said, "Del Eggers could come in mighty handy. He might manage it so that nobody would get shot. I'd as soon we didn't have to butt heads with Matt Wyatt, if there's any way of avoiding it."

"All right. Go after him. And send somebody to tell Frank Avila's old lady what's going on. If she can round up some friends of Frank's, tell

185

her to have 'em meet us at the depot in half an hour."

"Sure, boss." Dutch picked Domingo Sanchez to ride to the Avila house, because Sanchez spoke Spanish fluently and would probably be trusted more than an Anglo would. He and Sanchez spurred their horses and galloped on ahead of the others. Sanchez cut right short of the tracks and rode toward the Mexican settlement. Dutch pulled his horse back to a walk and headed for the Eggers house.

It was next door to the parsonage, the windows of which were dark. A single lamp burned in the Eggers parlor. Dutch tied his horse, went up the gravel walk to the door and knocked. It opened almost immediately, and Del Eggers stood framed in it. Dutch said, "Del, I've got to talk to you."

"All right. Come on in." Eggers stood aside and Dutch Hahn went in.

Mrs. Eggers was sitting in a rocker beside the table, evidence of tears plainly visible in her eyes. Dutch took off his hat and stood just inside the door, turning it around and around in his hands. Del Eggers asked, "What is it, Dutch?"

"Olaf and the crew are down at the depot. They're going to break the boys out of jail. I'm going with them to Mexico to make sure they get there all right. I'll have two or three of the crew with me."

Eggers looked stunned for a moment. Then hope flashed briefly in his eyes. It faded and he said angrily, "You know I'm Matt's deputy. What the hell are you telling me this for? Now I got to. . . ."

This had concerned Dutch. He said, "Don't you think I know? I just figured maybe you were a father first and a deputy after that."

Mrs. Eggers said pleadingly, "Del. . . ." She didn't finish. Her hands lay in her lap, hard clenched, the knuckles showing white.

Eggers was silent a moment. Then he said, "What will they do in Mexico? They'll be outlaws. They can never come back, not as long as they live."

"That just ain't so, Del. Sol Shapiro and Olaf are going to see to it that the boys get along all right. And when this has blown over — maybe in a year — the boys can come back into the States. What if they can't come back here? At least they won't hang. At least they won't rot away their lives in a stinking prison cell."

He could see evidences of the battle raging inside Del Eggers' mind. He didn't know how it was going to come out, but if Del didn't agree to join them, Dutch meant to see to it that he couldn't interfere. The silence dragged, the tension building up visibly in Del as the seconds ticked away. Mrs. Eggers said pleadingly, "Del, please. He's our boy."

Del looked at her. Dutch's eye caught movement in the doorway, and he saw Josie, in her nightgown, standing there. She said nothing and she did not come into the room. She was watching her father's face as though she was hypnotized.

At last Del Eggers' shoulders slumped. "All right. What do you want me to do?"

"You can get into the jail. You can put a gun on Matt. That way, we won't have to shoot it out with him. Maybe we can get it all done without anybody getting hurt." He glanced at Josie again. He knew she and Matt had been going together. Was her loyalty to Matt the greater, or was her loyalty to her brother paramount? It didn't matter, he supposed. He didn't see how she could reach Matt Wyatt to warn him in time. He said, "Olaf and the crew are down at the depot. Domingo Sanchez went to see Mrs. Avila. You go to the jail. We'll give you twenty minutes to get inside and put a gun on Matt."

Eggers nodded. He went to the closet and got a light coat. He took his holstered gun and cartridge belt from the coat tree and buckled it around his waist. Mrs. Eggers said, "Be careful, Del."

He nodded shortly and started for the door. Her voice very soft, Mrs. Eggers said, "And God take care of you."

Dutch stepped out onto the porch. Eggers came out immediately behind, pulling the door closed as he did. Dutch said, "Your daughter heard. Will she try to give us away?"

"Don't worry about her. Twenty minutes."

Dutch grunted assent. By the time he had untied his horse and mounted him, Eggers was already half a block away, walking swiftly toward the jail. Holding the horse to a walk, Dutch headed back down the street toward the railroad tracks.

Eggers was torn by conflicting emotions as he hurried toward the jail. He was terrified for Carl, and knew that even if he wasn't hanged, the boy would spend many years of his life in prison. To all intents and purposes, Carl's life was at an end. Even if he wasn't a criminal in the usual sense when he entered the prison, he would be one when he came out.

That Carl had participated in the attack on Daisy, and later in the beating of Arnold Means, Eggers didn't doubt. But, like Olaf Gunderson, he knew who had really killed Arnold Means. He knew it had been Orvie Gunderson. He had seen some of Orvie's rages himself, and he could imagine what had happened in that alley last night. What really surprised him was that neither Frank Avila nor Carl had stopped Orvie before it was too late.

Walking down Kansas Street, the block and a half between the hotel and the jail, he felt an overpowering uneasiness. He tried to tell himself the uneasiness was caused by guilt over what he was about to do, but he didn't entirely accept that explanation of it. He glanced nervously to right and left, not seeing anything. Once he heard a noise, but when he looked toward the source of it, he could see nothing, and decided it must have been made by a night-prowling cat.

He reached the jail and knocked. Matt Wyatt opened the door and Eggers stepped inside. Wyatt closed the door behind him and bolted it, then turned his head to look at Del.

He didn't question Del's motives for being here. He apparently had assumed that Del had been notified of what was happening, and had come on down to help.

Eggers studied Wyatt's face. Bertram Means and his brother Lane were just behind Wyatt, watching Eggers suspiciously. It wasn't going to be easy to get the drop on all three of them, he thought, but maybe when Gunderson and his crew actually approached the jail, Wyatt and the Means brothers would have their attention diverted long enough for him to manage it. He asked, "How is he, Matt?"

Wyatt said, "I expect he's pretty scared."

Eggers glanced at Bertram Means and then at Lane. "He's not a bad kid."

Neither man's expression softened.

Eggers' face flushed. He said, "You both have kids. I just hope nothing like this ever happens to you."

Bertram said angrily, "My boy wouldn't. . . ." He stopped suddenly.

Eggers said, "I didn't think my boy would ever do anything like this either. You both know him, and you both know me. You know his ma and me raised him right."

Bertram's expression softened for the first

time. Gruffly he said, "Nobody's blamin' you."

Wyatt interrupted the dialogue. "Never mind that now. We got plenty to worry about without fixing blame." He turned his back on Del Eggers and walked to the window. Putting up both hands to shut out the light, he peered through the glass.

He stood at the window for a long time, straining his eyes, trying to see if anything was moving outside in the street. But his mind wasn't in the street. It was on Del Eggers, his deputy. Nobody had said anything about telling Del what was going on. Del, therefore, had no way of knowing Gunderson was going to attack the jail, unless Gunderson or one of his men had let him know.

If they had, then Del would try putting a gun on him. He'd try to take over inside the jail to lessen the possibility of someone getting shot.

He stepped back from the window. He said, "They must all be in place. I can't see a thing."

He studied Del's face covertly as he spoke, and saw the surprise in it. Del hadn't known about the townsmen out in the street, waiting in ambush for Gunderson and his crew, which proved it had been Gunderson who had sent him there. It also proved that sooner or later Del would try to get the drop on him.

He heard a pounding on the door, a frantic pounding that sent him to it hurrying. He slammed back the bolt, knowing even as he did, that no man stood in the street outside. That knock had been a woman's knock.

As he expected, Josie Eggers stood there in the door, wearing a wrapper over her nightgown. Her hair was in braids for the night. He had never seen her so, and found the way she looked very appealing. She glanced beyond him at her father, then asked breathlessly, "May I come in?"

Wyatt stood aside. "Sure. Come in." He looked steadily at Del Eggers' face. Josie said, "I'm sorry, Pa. But it isn't right. You know it isn't right."

He nodded, his face suddenly very tired and old. He said, "I was supposed to get the drop on you, Matt. Then I was supposed to let Gunderson and Shapiro in. They were going to take Carl along with them to Mexico."

Wyatt said, "It wouldn't have worked. There are fifteen or twenty men waiting out there for Gunderson and his crew to show."

Eggers asked, "Do you want me to leave?"

Wyatt said, "You're my deputy. I need you here."

There was gratitude in Eggers' eyes. Wyatt said, "Josie, you go on home."

Her eyes begged him to let her stay, but he shook his head. Obediently she went to the door.

Wyatt followed her and opened it. She looked up at him, scared and trembling. There was something in her eyes he had never seen there before, something he had never seen in any woman's eyes. She said softly, "Be careful, Matt.

If anything happened to you. . . ."

He bent and kissed her lightly on the mouth. "It's going to be all right."

She nodded, not believing it, and frightened still. But she went out and headed uptown toward home, occasionally looking back fearfully.

He watched her until she was out of sight. Then he turned his attention to the buildings across the street. He could see nothing at first, but he finally made out the movement of one man's darker shape against the sky. They were in place, waiting.

He looked down toward the depot, seeing nothing, hearing nothing. Gunderson's men would come quickly and confidently, he thought, expecting no resistance, expecting that Eggers would be in control of the jail.

Something had to be done immediately to change things. If it wasn't, the next few minutes might be a bloodbath. He opened his mouth to yell at the men across the street, but he was too late. Gunderson's crew came thundering up the street at full gallop, and his shout was lost in the noise they made. He jumped back, slammed the door and bolted it. He turned, hearing as he did the shattering of glass back in the cells, and shortly afterward the thunder of a gun.

Out in the street, that gunshot was echoed by a whole volley of them. Wyatt was already running toward the door leading to the cells in the rear. He slammed it open and rushed down the corridor to the door Shoemaker had built into the partition.

Behind him in the office there was silence. He slammed open the wooden door and looked into Daisy's cell.

She was lying on her cot, cowering, pressed against the stone wall beneath the window. On the floor, illuminating the cell, was a stick, around one end of which rags had been wrapped. Soaked in coal oil and ignited, it made a torch, which had been thrust through the shattered window into Daisy's cell.

Framed by the broken window, Wyatt saw the face of a man, and he saw a poised and ready gun. The gun leveled and belched fire, and the bullet slammed into the wooden partition beside Wyatt's head, showering him with splinters.

He automatically grabbed his own gun, leveled it, and fired at the face. It disappeared instantly. He thought his bullet had struck, but he wasn't absolutely sure.

Daisy was weeping now, hysterically, with pure terror. Wyatt unlocked the cell, went in, and stamped out the torch. He said soothingly, "Stay where you are, Daisy. It's going to be all right."

Retreating, he locked the door of her cell again. The boys across the corridor were standing at the bars. He ran back to the office, slamming the door behind him as he did.

A bullet shattered the window, covering the floor with shards of broken glass. Wyatt sent the

194

lamp sailing across the room with a single sweep of his arm. It broke against the wall, leaving the room wholly dark.

There now was utter turmoil outside in the street. To Wyatt, it sounded like a battle was going on, and he wondered how many now would have to die because last night four wild kids had lost their heads.

CHAPTER

20

Bertram and Lane Means were crouched against the wall at the rear of the room. Del Eggers stood beside the broken window, a shotgun in his hands. Wyatt crossed the room, stood beside him, and peered into the street.

The gunfire had died as abruptly as it had begun. For a few moments, the horses, abandoned by Gunderson and his crew, milled confusedly in the streets. Then, one led off galloping toward the railroad tracks, and the others turned and followed him. In moments, even the sounds of their galloping hoofs had died away.

Eggers asked softly, "Now what?"

"Hell, I don't know. Maybe Gunderson will back off. He knows he's walked into a trap."

"Not Gunderson. He and his boys just took cover. We ain't seen the last of them."

Wyatt said, "One of them tried to kill Daisy."

"Uh-huh. I heard you shoot. Did you hit him?"

"Could have." In the darkness Wyatt grinned.

"Or he could just had pulled his head back real quick."

Suddenly the gunfire in the street began again, but it was different this time. It was slow and measured, as if each man who fired had a definite target at which to shoot. Wyatt heard a high yell of pain from one man who had been hit. He said, "They'll pull back. Gunderson's men are too much for them."

"You think they'll quit?"

"I think they already have. When they thought they had the advantage, they were brave enough. But with accurate fire coming at them from Gunderson's men, they haven't got the stomach for it."

"Then Gunderson's going to be coming here. There's nothing to stop him now."

Wyatt nodded. In his mind he asked himself if he could shoot point blank into Gunderson's crew as they broke through the door, and he knew that he could not. He knew too many of them personally, and he knew what they were doing was done out of simple loyalty to their boss. They didn't deserve to die for that.

He said, "Gimme that shotgun."

"What the hell do you think you're going to do?"

"I'm going after Gunderson. That's the only way this can be stopped, by getting him."

"You'll never get close to him. Wait for him to come to you."

Wyatt shook his head. "That'll be too late. By

the time he gets here to the door, his crew will be right behind. They'll come on even if Gunderson goes down."

He unbolted the door and opened it a crack. He peered outside. Behind him he heard Del Eggers' voice, soft, incredulous, "You'd trust me with the jail? After what I came down here to do?"

Wyatt said, "Bolt the door after me." He glanced across the room at the Means brothers. They got sheepishly to their feet when they saw him looking at them. He doubted if Eggers could shoot into Gunderson's crew if they came all together as a mob and broke down the door. He knew the Means brothers could not.

Which left it squarely up to him. Unless he could get Gunderson, the jail was going to be taken. The boys would be released. Daisy would probably be killed.

He stepped out into the street, instantly moving along the wall to the corner of the building. Shotgun poked ahead of him, he rounded the corner, ready to shoot if he ran into anyone. He did not. The lot was vacant, or at least it seemed to be.

Somehow he had to locate Gunderson, and he knew that wasn't going to be easy in the dark. The only possible way was to move confidently, as if he was one of Gunderson's crew. In the darkness they wouldn't shoot, because they wouldn't be sure enough of his identity.

He ran across the vacant lot, the weeds rustling beneath his feet. He saw a shadow ahead and to the right, and veered instantly toward it. He knew the man might shoot, but he also knew it was a chance he'd have to take. Making his voice into an urgent whisper, he croaked, "Where the hell is Gunderson?"

"Other side of the jail." There was a pause as Wyatt veered away, still moving fast. Then the man's voice came again, "Say! Who the hell are you?"

Wyatt didn't answer him. He ducked in against the wall of the jail, into the shadows there. He almost bowled another man over as he collided with him. The man went to one knee with a muffled curse, but Wyatt didn't stop. He ran on, rounding the back corner of the jail and plunging on.

A shot racketed in the street, and then there was silence once again. Wyatt had a desperate feeling that time was slipping away from him. Gunderson must know by now that the townsmen had retreated from their vantage points. He would move on the jail, and he would move fast before they could reorganize.

Reaching the far back corner of the jail, Wyatt called in his urgent whisper, "They're out, Mr. Gunderson! Where you at?"

The vacant lot on this side of the jail was littered with boards and trash, and beyond was a deserted building that had once housed a saloon. Behind it was a dilapidated shed. In front of the shed there was movement, and Wyatt called again, "Mr. Gunderson!"

He heard Gunderson's reply, harsh and short, and called in his urgent whisper, "They're out, Mr. Gunderson! The boys are out! They're over here!"

Gunderson's voice queried harshly, "Del? Is that you?"

Wyatt didn't reply directly to that. He veered away, still running, heading now for the alley. Over his shoulder he called back, "Over here!"

He reached the alley and turned north, toward the shadows behind the stable in which he kept his horse. He halted suddenly, turning to face the direction from which Gunderson would come.

How many of Gunderson's crew would come along with him, he had no idea. If more than one or two came, he was dead. But he figured Gunderson would leave Dutch Hahn behind to keep an eye on the jail, in case this turned out to be a trick. And he figured Gunderson would leave most of his men with Hahn.

He heard the pounding of running feet, and suddenly saw the bulky shape of Gunderson come into the alley from the vacant lot. He thumbed both hammers back and waited, his finger curled over the front trigger of the gun.

One man was behind Gunderson, keeping pace, but about ten yards behind. When the big man was only a dozen paces away, Wyatt called sharply, "Hold it, Mr. Gunderson. Hold it right there and drop your gun."

Gunderson halted, but he didn't drop his gun. He set himself, feet spread and planted solidly as he peered ahead, trying to pierce the shadows in which Wyatt stood.

Wyatt held his fire. He had deliberately placed himself here in the shadow of the stable to put Gunderson at a disadvantage. He didn't want to shoot the man, and he figured if Gunderson couldn't see him, he wouldn't risk shooting it out with him.

But he had been wrong. Gunderson raised his gun to his shoulder. . . .

Wyatt didn't know what kind of gun he had. If it was a rifle, there was little chance he would be hit. But if it was a shotgun, he didn't have a chance.

He didn't hesitate. He flung himself forward, falling, keeping his own gun extended before him so that he could fire it from the ground.

Gunderson's gun roared, belching smoke and fire, unmistakably a shotgun, and a big bore shotgun at that. Wyatt knew he could wait no longer. Gunderson still had a barrel left, and it was now obvious he would kill the sheriff if he could. He had come this far, and now would not go back.

Wyatt fired from the ground, knowing, even as he pulled the trigger, that he hadn't missed.

He saw Gunderson driven back, as violently as if he had been struck by something big and solid. The man sprawled on his back in the alley and didn't move.

The cloud of powdersmoke from Wyatt's shotgun rolled out, and for an instant obscured the man who had been directly behind Gunderson. Scrambling frantically across the alley, Wyatt roared, "Drop your gun, or you get the other one!"

The man was set, spraddle-legged, ready to back up his boss. But the cloud of powdersmoke made it impossible for him to see, and besides, his boss was dead, and this demoralized him more than anything else could have done. He yelled frantically, "All right! All right!" and flung his gun away from him.

Wyatt got to his feet. He said, "Get Hahn and the rest of your boys and take Mr. Gunderson home."

He didn't wait to see if he would be obeyed. He knew Hahn might even now be mounting an assault against the front of the jail. Running, he plowed through the litter and trash, heading toward the street.

He could see a group of men over against the abandoned saloon next door. He yelled, "Dutch?"

"What?"

"Your boss is dead. He's back in the alley. Get him, and get the hell out of here before anybody else gets hurt."

He had no idea where Shapiro was, but the banker didn't worry him. He ran on, still not sure everything was all right in the jail. He had trusted Del Eggers and had left him in charge.

But Del had been a father a long time before he had been a deputy.

Rounding the building, he called, "Del, it's me. Open up."

The door gaped open and he plunged inside. He still had a charge in his gun, but he had eased the hammer back down, not wanting it to discharge accidentally. The door slammed behind him, and he stood there in the darkness, panting, his back to the wall.

Slowly, he let the gun sag to his side. He had killed Gunderson, but he wasn't going to kill anybody else. No matter what they did. He said, "Is everything all right?"

Eggers said, "Sure. You knew it would be, didn't you?"

Wyatt felt the breath sigh out of him. He said, "Del, maybe it won't be so bad. Maybe we can get the county attorney to settle for a manslaughter charge."

Eggers did not reply.

Wyatt said, "It's better than Mexico. They'd have turned outlaw, sure as hell."

"I know they would."

Wyatt said, "Gunderson's dead. The trouble's over with." He turned his head and looked at Bertram and Lane. "You two can leave. Thanks for your help." He fumbled for a match and lighted another lamp.

Bertram looked embarrassed. Passing Del Eggers, he stopped. "We won't push this thing, Mr. Eggers. Whatever the county attorney says, is all right with us. We've got kids too."

Del nodded, unable to look up. Bertram and Lane went out.

Del looked at Wyatt. "Can I talk to him?"

"Sure. Go on back."

Eggers opened the door at the rear of the room and went into the corridor. He closed the door behind him.

Wyatt opened the front door and stepped out onto the walk. There was the smell of rain in the air. A block up the street Brock Davidson was locking up the saloon for the night.

Twenty-four hours, Wyatt thought. It seemed like that many years. Josie Eggers came running down the street, nightgown and braids flying. He waited for her, knowing suddenly that as soon as the trial was over with he would marry her. Kiowa would never be the same. Neither would he. But life went on. Fortunately, life went on.

The employees of G.K. Hall hope you have enjoyed this Large Print book. All our Large Print titles are designed for easy reading, and all our books are made to last. Other G.K. Hall books are available at your library, through selected bookstores, or directly from us.

For information about titles, please call:

(800) 223-1244
(800) 223-6121

To share your comments, please write:

Publisher
G.K. Hall & Co.
P.O. Box 159
Thorndike, ME 04986